Stinging Fly Patrons

Many thanks to: Mark Armstrong, Maria Behan, Niamh Black, John Boyne, Trish Byrne, Edmond Condon, Evelyn Conlon, Sean Curran, Edel Fairclough, Michael J. Farrell, Ciara Ferguson, Olivia Gaynor-Long, Michael Gillen, Brendan Hackett, James Hanley, Christine Dwyer Hickey, Dennis Houlihan, Peggy Hughes, Nuala Jackson, Geoffrey Keating, Jack Keenan, Jerry Kelleher, John Kelleher, Conor Kennedy, Gráinne Killeen, Joe Lawlor, Irene Rose Ledger, Róisín McDermott, Petra McDonough, Lynn Mc Grane, Jon McGregor, Finbar McLoughlin, Maggie McLoughlin, Ama, Grace & Fraoch MacSweeney, Mary MacSweeney, Paddy & Moira MacSweeney, Anil Malhotra, Gerry Marmion, Dáirine Ní Mheadhra, Mary O'Donnell, Lucy Perrem, Maria Pierce, Peter J. Pitkin, Mark Richards, Fiona Ruff, Alf Scott, Ann Seery, Eileen Sheridan, Alfie & Savannah Stephenson, Mike Timms, Colleen Toomey, Olive Towey, Simon Trewin, Debbi Voisey, Ruth Webster, Lilliput Press, Poetry Ireland and Tramp Press.

We'd also like to thank those individuals who have expressed the preference to remain anonymous.

By making an annual contribution of 75 euro, patrons provide us with vital support and encouragement.

Become a patron online at
www.stingingfly.org
or send a cheque or postal order to:
The Stinging Fly, PO Box 6016, Dublin 1.

New Writers, New Writing
The Stinging Fly
Issue 35 · Volume Two · Winter 2016-17 · €10.00/£8.00
Fear & Fantasy

| 5 | Mia Gallagher | Editorial |

NEW FICTION

10	Luke Sheehan	*The House of Love*
20	Lucy Sweeney Byrne	*To Cure a Body*
31	Ronan Flaherty	*Re-Animator Tales*
36	Trevor Fevin	*Forrester*
48	Olivia Heal	*The Guinea Fowl*
50	Clara Kumagai	*Real Boys*
57	Roisín O'Donnell	*The Great Hunger*
66	Brendan Murphy	*The Fire at the Ritz*
92	Ian Shine	*Cute*
94	Anne Griffin	*The Boy who Left*
105	Darragh Cotter	*For Silence*
115	James B.L. Hollands	*Just What's For You, You'll Get It*
124	Oliver Arnoldi	*Katharine*
137	Heather Parry	*Amelia Magdalene*
146	Oran Ryan	*Joe the Aquanaut and the Aftermath Blue*

NEW POEMS

18	Niamh Prior	*Dr Jekyll*
19	Gerard Hanberry	*Freckles*
29	Caroline Hardaker	*Gums*
30	Jonathan Greenhause	*The ghost was not a normal one*
41	Nessa O'Mahony	*Bogeyman*
49	Alex Harper	*The Trade*
56	Rachel Plummer	*Dollhouse*
65	Natasha Calder	*Troll Song*
75	Patrick Cotter	*The Town of Checkers*
93	Susan Millar DuMars	*In His Attic*
101	Simon Lewis	*I was your Golem*
102	Dave Rudden	*Rambda Runs on Reddened Wheels*
104	Jennie Taylor	*There Is A Risk of Decay*

NEW POEMS (CONTINUED)

113	Dawn Watson	*Creep*
114	David McLoghlin	*Mixed Media*
122	Paul McMahon	*Milltown Cemetery, Belfast, March 16th, 1988*
136	Evan Costigan	*The Shroud*
144	Jane Robinson	*Radium Mother*
145	Matthew Sweeney	*The Blind Clairvoyant*

FICTION IN TRANSLATION

| 76 | Vladimir Poleganov | *The Feather* (translated from the Bulgarian by Peter Bachev) |

NEW TRANSDISCIPLINARY

Maeve O'Lynn (text)   *The Xenophon Tapes*
& Siobhán McGibbon (images)   Pages 8-9, 46-47, 90-91 & 134-135

ESSAYS

42	Rachel Sneyd	*Dead Baby v Dead Baby*
86	Bernice Murphy	*Short, Sharp Shocks*
130	Philip St John	Re:fresh	*House of Leaves* by Mark Z. Danielewski

COVER ART

Gary Coyle   *Hello Darkness*

COVER DESIGN

Fergal Condon

'... God has specially appointed me to this city, so as though it were a large thoroughbred horse which because of its great size is inclined to be lazy and needs the stimulation of some stinging fly...'

—Plato, *The Last Days of Socrates*

The Stinging Fly
new writers, new writing

Issue Guest Editor
Mia Gallagher

Publisher/Editor
Declan Meade

Design & Layout
Fergal Condon

Assistant Editor
Fiona Boyd

Poetry Editor
Eabhan Ní Shúileabháin

Eagarthóir filíochta Gaeilge
Aifric MacAodha

Contributing Editors
Emily Firetog, Dave Lordan, Thomas Morris & Sean O'Reilly

© Copyright remains with authors and artists, 2016

Printed by Naas Printing Ltd, County Kildare
ISBN 978-1-906539-58-0   ISSN 1393-5690

The Stinging Fly gratefully acknowledges the support of The Arts Council/ An Chomhairle Ealaíon and Dublin City Council

PO Box 6016, Dublin 1
stingingfly@gmail.com

Keep in touch: sign up to our e-mail newsletter, become a fan on Facebook, or follow us on Twitter for regular updates about all publications, events and activities.

www.stingingfly.org | www.facebook.com/StingingFly | @stingingfly

Editorial

O God, says Hamlet to his treacherous school buddies, Rosencrantz and Guildenstern, I could be bounded in a nutshell and count myself the king of infinite space, were it not that I have bad dreams.

Do other animals dream? I don't know. But we do. We dream at night and in daytime; of good things and bad. Our dreams are ferocious, consuming, titillating, arousing. Terrifying. Sticks to beat ourselves with or opiate promises to dull the pain of the present. Some of us put our dreams into words or sounds or pictures or movements and the rest of the world calls this art. There is art which is realistic and representational. It feels familiar. Hah, we say: there's the world as I know it. And then there's the other kind. Strange, new, startling—yet familiar too, as known to us as our own guts.

Francis Bacon prized sensation: if his work didn't affect the viewer's nervous system, he didn't think it was any good. There is a horrific quality, I think, to his paintings. They affect me the way works of the frightening and the fantastical have affected me since I was a child. That weird 1920s black-and-white movie I glimpsed on the telly, where a body got stretched so thin it became a worm; Maupassant's *Le Horla* (read, bad idea, at age 9); Heathcliff's Cathy tapping the midnight window of *Wuthering Heights*; Barney's legs sliced through, bone and all, by a spinning wire in RTE's *Strumpet City*; and, most recently, Jeff Vandermeer's strange, creepily urgent sci-fi novel *Annihilation*.

Every one of us has a lexicon of horror, a set of touchstones we use to measure and contain our fear. In editing this issue, while being informed by my own lexicon, I've also had the privilege of being flooded by the fear-vocabulary of hundreds of other people. I've met their werewolves, vampires, witches and ghosts; their self-obsessed weirdos; their nightmarish holding rooms. I've encountered their clawed metamorphs and creepy haunted houses. Seen blood flow, skin pierced, soft openings brutalised. I've heard bones and hearts break, tasted human flesh, been buried alive. And the loneliness—oh my god, I've felt the loneliness.

This issue began as an idea. A collection of dark fairy tales, inspired by Deirdre Gleeson's deeply disturbing vampire/banshee horror, 'Daragh Maguire and the

Black Blood', in the 2008 Stinging Fly anthology *Let's Be Alone Together*. It was the story I would have loved to write and I couldn't help wondering if there were more of these beauties lurking around in the Irish subconscious. As the conversations with Declan Meade and the Fly team unfolded, the creature started to shift shape. Why restrict it to Irish writers writing about Irish themes? Why just stories? Why not make it a special issue, featuring poetry and essays too? As for focus, fairy tales would be great, but what about the Gothic? Or body horror? Or—ooh, a ghost story or two? Declan came up with a working title—Fear & Fantasy. Perfect. And with 'fantasy', open season started. Because, of course, there was all that other stuff I've hoarded on my shelves since I first entered Narnia. High-fantasy, sci-fi, surrealism…

Sean O'Reilly has spoken of how a journal issue, like any piece of work, doesn't know what it is when it starts off. I had assumed editing would be straightforward—you picks the ones you like, throw a couple of punctuation suggs to the writers, and hey presto. Last winter, the submissions started slouching towards us. In April, I began reading—all 250-plus stories and around sixty poems that Eabhan had expertly winnowed out for me. I want you to pick ones you love, I'd emailed her. But also the ones that make you feel horrible.

From the start the stories had me in reading heaven. Each brushed off the theme in some way, and many were underscored by a joyous, affectionate nod towards the genre/s. I scribbled a terse note on every cover page, nearly all some variant of 'liked this!', 'ooh!' or 'euwww—fab.' Some were simply 'I <u>LOVE</u> this'.

Straightforward? How wrong my initial assumption was. I was finding it really hard to say No. So I colour-coded the stories into eight shades of Yes gradating all the way down to Possibly(?). Still hundreds in the pile. Utilising a more rational approach, I grouped them into sub-genre: magic, faerie, vampires, sci-fi, surrealist, body horror, myth, solipsism, apocalypse, nihilism and—my favourite—monsters & metamorphs.

Rationality, ultimately, wasn't much help. As the essayists in this issue persuasively argue, works of horror and fantasy are stabs at a particular type of meaning-making. Trying to plumb the depths of what makes me—or you—or us—afraid and put a strange new shape on it. When the shape created by the writer bumps into what's hiding in the reader's basement, meaning happens. In the end, I chose the stories that, when I'd read them or thought about them afterwards, I loved the most. The ones I'd scribbled on with those capital letters, underlined three times. The ones that wouldn't leave me alone. The poems I selected later, to cluster around the prose like small dark gems. How funny, that in an issue dedicated to fear, it was love which was my magnet—triangulated by the sense that I needed to select pieces I hadn't seen before, pieces that felt to me truly strange, or weird, or even just *odd*. Rilke wrote beautifully about dragons and princesses: how the things that most terrify us are the things we need to pay most attention to. Jung spoke about the shadow: the dark shape lurking in our psyche that embodies all the stuff we don't think we are. The 39 pieces of writing featured here are the ones which speak most to my shadow, which bring my dragon out from hiding so he can show me my sad, soft-bellied princess.

You will notice that most of them are written in the first person, that they're set in the present or a recentish past or a kind of future. That none of them are what you'd call pure genre: horror or sci-fi or surrealism or supernatural, but each has echoes of these forms somewhere in their mix. In his last editorial, Thomas Morris talked about repetition and resonance, and I can't help that my fears follow grooves. You'll spot a lot of monsters and shape-shifters, an unsettling amount of female victims, a few dead babies, and Wolves, of course (I've a thing for Wolves). The original kernel, dark fairy-tales, have made their way in too. Look closely and you'll find Goldilocks, twisted Cinderellas, a Troll, Bluebeard, a witch or two, several warped FrankenJekyllstein wizards, and Pinocchio. Then there are the scary fairy-tales of our own age—radiation poisoning, rising sea-levels, AIDS, genetic modification, fundamentalist religion, nationalism gone mad, cancer. And the twin pulses of that sad princess's beating heart: isolation and depression.

Bacon would approve, I think. Every piece in this issue—and here I include Siobhán McGibbon's creepy visual delicacies and (fangirl moment) Gary Coyle's iconic cover art—has made me feel something. Repulsion, pity, exhilaration. Humour. That nasty sensation on the back of my neck that tells me I'm in the presence of a real Monster. I've been startled and moved, sometimes to tears. I've wanted to stop reading while compelled to keep going. I've been uplifted, not just by the glorious writing of these abundantly talented contributors, but by the tiny, luminous grains of transcendence—hope? they offer from the darkness. Enjoy the dreaming. Seek out those shadows. And may your dragons ever rise to meet you.

Mia Gallagher
Dublin, October 2016

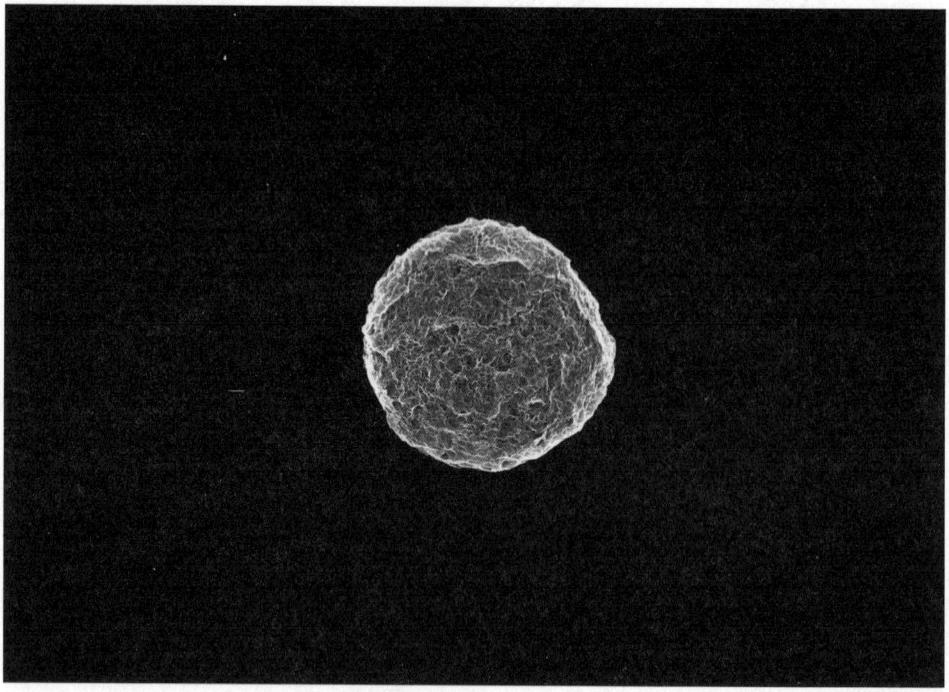

Introduction: The Xenophon Tapes

Little concrete data survives from the world as it was, the world before the Incident. *History has become vague, causation uncertain.*

From the fragments here assembled, now known as **The Xenophon Tapes**, we have been able to infer the following.

In 2028 a study was commissioned by an anonymous consortium, led by R'lyeh University, a private research institute in Switzerland. The precise nature, size and aims of this study remain unknown, as does the identity of the consortium that commissioned and funded the research.

The study's results were made public in 2035. It was widely believed at the time that the results that were made public were only a small fraction of the body of research undertaken.

In 2040, the **Xenophon** was first revealed.

Medical science was rocked to its core and great advancements in curing disease and vastly prolonging human life were predicted.

Para-Humans – that which humans had now become – had achieved near invincibility. Yet that which made us stronger became our ultimate weakness. From even the greatest of horrors irony is seldom absent.

In 2093 society collapsed. It has not yet recovered.

Presented to the sub-committee hearing for the first time in their entirety, please find enclosed **The Xenophon Tapes**. Make your own deductions accordingly.

Those who do not learn history are doomed to repeat it.

The world is indeed comic, but the joke is on mankind.

[Ends]/

FUTURE RELIC ONE: SPHERES
Content: Origins and results of apocryphal R'lyeh Study 1-890.

Incomplete fragment of recording.

In 2025, analogue radio signal was switched off in the UK. Many radio listeners did not have access to the new DAB signal. Conspiracy theories ran rife that the British government had made this decision to silence discussion and dissent. Pirate stations became widespread, broadcasting on FM from temporary locations which

The House of Love
Luke Sheehan

It was the start of the end of the House of His Love. We had come to a place with no name. The sun was going down. On a headland in the distance there were men who had come from the sea. They had risen there as vague little shapes. With my bad eyes I was late to perceive them as men. The shadows sprouted arms and legs and my novice, Donn, pushed me down and we lay there flat. The outlines grew larger, shrank, grew again. We watched them, and I felt His Love escape from the world. We were quiet and still, keeping flat on the grass. My chin was on a rock, and Donn's hand was on his knife. Over the waves, the seabirds were calling. The men moved closer together. One of them gestured at the sky, towards the cold white sun. It was impossible to say what their ages were, though one of them was fat, and had long white hair like a woman's which flowed above his head in the wind. He stood apart from the others, sulking.

I felt that the world was a drum which was pounded once or twice.

They disappeared off out of view, perhaps to the beach, we thought to a small boat, which they would row back to their ship, which would be hidden in a cave. If that was what it was, they did not get into it. They did not go back to join another ship and they did not go back to the north, where they were from, although the truth was we had all come farther north than was sensible. Instead, they returned to the headland and spent the night in a hollow there. We followed. When they settled down, we walked on our elbows and knees to hide in a niche in the rock to try to hear what they were saying. We couldn't understand it. I could hear Donn's heart beating. We retreated for several hours and discussed what to do. We argued. We spoke through our teeth. He wanted to count their number. To be sure.

We climbed back to the same patch. We saw smoke and a tiny tongue of flame. We were envious of the fire, but there would be no going up to it. He wanted to attack them while they slept. Not possible. Too many bodies were moving on the flame.

I said, 'Let's go.'

But Donn was watching them, and his hands were tearing at the grass.

*

It was a period of months after disease and despair had ruined our home: two years after my thirtieth year alive. Two years since white strangers had first come to make a hecatomb out of our nearest community of neighbours, and our House, built for His Love, into a hiding place where we waited to be found.

We remained there through the winters, waiting, thinking about the old country where the sun rose and fell once a day. On this island, the extreme edge of the world, the winters took the sun from the sky and no light existed except for the light of candles and fires. In the New Year, with the short days finally breaking on the water, Donn and I were chosen for a period of keeping watch and hunting, moving west along the shores until we gradually reached the north. This was work that would last until until the next dividing day when the moon and sun shone for the same length of time. It would bring us where ice floes ran in the distance, where nobody lived or fished.

It was here the strangers had landed first. They must have been ravenous by the time they made it to the green parts. In the community nearest to us, they had killed every man over the age of twelve and every child under the age of three. They had taken the women, but for one or two grandmothers whom they left in the ashes. Later a child was found inland, wearing a mask, trying to keep warm by the heat of the fumes from a vent. The survivor, who did not speak real words, was taken in and made into a novice, to work with Carick, binding and restoring books in the workshop. He showed love for the substances used in these processes, and when he was finally dissuaded from assessing them with his tongue, learned their names and became proficient in their use.

*

In the night, Donn panted. He wanted to decapitate white strangers. I felt that in his dreams, as we lay wrapped in sealskin by the smoking ash, he heard the air whistle from throats as he cut them open. He was probably smiling, in his skins, as the red juice jetted and pumped from the neck, dripping and splashing while he carved through the hinge of skin to remove the head. He wanted to hold the head up, dedicate this act to His Love and attach it, by a rope run through the ears, to a post on a headland, or on a chain attached to the post, the chain run through the skull to another post. To make a fence. Allowed to continue he would fence every beach, until he ran out of coast, or out of skulls.

Donn was earmarked by His Love to die in his own way—the red way. And I was earmarked by His Love to die slowly, on my own—the white way, in a boat with books, floating towards the edge. And some others were earmarked by His Love to go the green way, on juts of stone out in the waves, eating seaweed and puffins, suffering every day, hearing the old bells in their heads, thinking no doubt of their mothers and brothers, in the old country.

But His Love went on working in our lives, and we went on singing.

*

On the return trip to make the alarm, we saw a white bear on a raft of ice, a short distance from the shore. Its tongue was dry. All it could do was wheeze. Behind it lay a cub, frozen. Donn swam to them, cut down the living bear and pulled both bodies onto the beach. I rubbed his hands and feet until he was warm again. He took the skin from the larger one and thawed the smaller one by the fire; when he had cut both skins off he turned them, that night, patch by patch by the flames, to half-cure the insides of the furs. We stood square sections of the shoulders on sticks by the flames and turned them about now and then and ate from them. They tasted bad. We were sick. I moved back and forth with more wood until I collapsed and slept. In the morning I found he had stitched the skins together with two upper jaws hanging off each shoulder. 'That's His Love,' I said. 'The two together, forever.'

'That was His Love,' he said. 'She wouldn't eat her cub although they were out there for who knows how long, and she starved beside her cub and did not even eat his tongue. Cub went the white way. She went the red way.'

We reached our House. There were forty-five living souls there and only His Love knew how many dead ones: it was a House that was heaving with flies in the summer, carpeted with rats in the autumn and shaken to the core, in the winter, by evil spirits. The ghosts of the Loveless and worse than that filled up the rooms to the roof and let no one sleep, taking the smoke from the candles and shaping it into grinning faces that dispersed near the ceilings. Periodic screams tore through the walls. We were jolted awake. If the noise persisted, the afflicted man would be encouraged to sleep alongside one of his brothers for comfort. On some occasions, despite searching, the screaming person could not be found. We loved our House, though, because His Love lived there, inside us. Almost always.

We were at the door. The slot was opened. A blue eye stared.

'You've been gone for seven days.'

'Did you miss us?'

'Put out your tongues.'

He scrutinised our tongues through the slot.

Then Donn lifted the head of the mother bear.

'Fuck!'

*

After we recounted what we had seen, the House shed every habitual and reassuring sound. Everyone prepared for Hell. Chickens and geese were shuffling faster, and the pigs screeched. Donn began to shove people aside so all the questions were addressed to me. As the group stood listening to my answers and asking me more questions, there was anger at the front of the crowd, and tragic noise, and at the back dumb confusion, and sadness.

Later I was alone, in the writing room, turning the pages of the Book.

The Book was reputed to sing or make a noise if evil approached. I put my head beside the page: I heard only my own breathing. It had arrived the summer before accompanied by a team of green-faced men, volunteers with enflamed anxieties about giant serpents and doors that opened down into hell, and equally absurd dreams of singing their way to the edge of the earth to peek out over it and see the messengers of His Love, hovering and whirling in a waterfall that would pour from the edge and pitch into the stars…

These boats had come less frequently over the last few summers. Sometimes a long boat full of different sorts of men, with a living leader. Other times smaller boats. One that washed up full of rags, feathers, dead birds, fish scales and many bones of different sizes, dried blood and shit, and the skull of someone. The human bones had been gnawed on by human teeth.

When the Book was first opened, the top pages were damp and a yellow larva was pumping inside the first word. Moths escaped it. There's more learning gone into them than into us, someone said. We put a lamp near the window, and so the learning flew away into the night.

Now the first pages had been repaired with our inferior inks. A red from seal's blood. Thin gold. The new binding was tight and carefully done. But it seemed to have lost the ability to sing. How could we put the power back into it?

*

Carick was the book-binder, though he couldn't be trusted to write. When we were singing, he stood at the back, smiling; he broke every note and had to be shushed. The same smile was stuck to him whether he was outside working or inside cleaning or making books. The youth, the survivor from the community, was learning maintenance from Carick, but it was thought unlikely that the training would lead the youngster into the garden of literacy.

Once a man denounced the boy. He was one of a group of visitors, a big boat, I forget his name. Many of us suspected, and some of us knew that this boy was likely not such, although he acted that way. The visitor said that His Law was not being followed. He went to check the sex. Carick went between them, took the man's ears and railed at him and then yanked one ear so the man fell. That was enjoyable. I'd never seen such a big man brought down by an ear.

*

The bell was rung. Everyone gathered. The Father of our House informed us all that we would soon be martyred: there was not much enthusiasm. Anyone who wanted to could leave, he said, and go to the island to the west, with the little house, and return after the attack; but no one volunteered.

We waited on our knees in the House of His Love for the strangers to come. We heard them at the gates. My eyes were shut. They came into the hall. They walked about, shouting even when they stood close together. They smelled of pure sea. I opened my eyes. In front of me was a handsome face, a bent nose and healed lip under thin hair, talking to a smaller man with a flat forehead and a leather cap tied to his skull. They had weapons in their hands, and more strapped to their backs or swinging by their sides. They ignored us. They walked in and out, gathering up our possessions and discussing their value.

They took all precious metals, any furs. A long basket of pelts was dragged away. Outside, they got to work on the barrels of food. They were interested in our bell, but argued about how to dislodge it. Our Father walked towards their leader and addressed him. The leader put a blade into our Father's heart and pulled it out, and then spun him around and held him so the blood poured out of him in our direction.

Finally, four of them were carrying the bell out through the gate, following the others. A group of three carried a locked chest. This was full of book materials. I went outside, walked around the perimeter, but couldn't see Donn. I went back to the gate. I climbed up the tower and looked out: they had left the bell on the rocks. Carick's voice was behind me. I turned. Carick was coming from the door of the House, following a stranger who carried the Book. He was grabbing for it. They kicked him out of the way. He was smiling. I climbed down.

Carick got up and followed them outside to the slope that led to the shore. I followed. Something made me turn and move along the cliffs instead.

I saw forms standing in a line on a headland. One of them was there with his arms raised. He uttered some words and the others answered together, and they kept on chanting as I approached. The lead chanter bent down and picked up two heavy objects and lifted them slowly. They were heads which he held by the ears. I recognised the dumb faces and the dropped jaws, and the pig-like underbites. Their expressions were not much changed from life. I felt sad but not so surprised. After all, Hell was inevitable and foreseen. For some time, we had been thinking of it every day. Then the holder of the heads saw me and made a remark, and I ran.

No one rushed to follow me.

*

Down by their ship, I saw the bell discarded in the surf. A group was loading our possessions onto the boat from a pile on the sand. Out by the keel, the fat one was held back with thin chains by two others, both of whom were shouting. They were shouting at Carick, who was running through the backwash with a wound in his side, holding the Book to his body. The chains were released. The fat one flew, tearing up the water. His eyes were agonised. On his helmet there was a sharp corner. He came to Carick, twisted Carick's face in his hands, pitched and butted him, then lifted his head and did it again, then dropped Carick into the water. The two behind him ran, grabbed the chains, and pulled the fat one backwards. His face was a parody of a baby's when it is first pulled out, a hallucination of hair and screaming. I saw the Book sinking and Carick floating with his temple bashed in, his eyes crossed like an idiot's and the ghost of the smile there. The fat one saw me staring. He was set free again. I could see down the black throat. The hair and the chains rose behind him as he jumped in the surf.

I moved. The earth beat.

*

When I got inside the gate, there were seven dead men lying in a line. Two were missing their heads. Three others were missing entirely. Carick, Donn and the youth from that community. I told what had happened by the boat. We stood at the wall and watched the vessel move out of the bay. There was going to be a storm: it was whispering over the grass. Everything was shapeless except for the water, which jumped and jerked and turned inside out like a god that couldn't decide which form to take.

We went to the beach. Someone heard a high singing sound and we followed it. We found the youth holding Carick's hand and babbling. The Book was on the chest of the body. The youth had put a cloth on the broken head. We put some cloaks on them. I carried the youth on my back and the others the body. At the House, there were many sounds—curses, blessings, questions. And quotations.

We went to reinforce things. The youth from the community, wrapped in his blanket at the top of the platform, gave a fierce cry. The boat had reappeared, retreating from the weather. The sail was attached on one side only and the untied corner writhed on their suffering bodies. Waves broke over them as they clung to the frame. Two oars were sticking out of the side of the boat, twitching. Then we could see a disturbance. We saw Donn with his back to the stern, holding a weapon. In his other hand he swung a head by the hair. The wind and the motion favoured him and the white strangers were falling on the deck, some of them cut by him and some knocked down by the storm. We shouted his name. The ship tilted over and the men spilled out of it. The sail lay on the water and it was lost.

*

The youth from the community was insane. We believed for a time that this was due to inhaling the fumes near the vents where he or she (because finally no one was quite sure which) had remained for a long time inland since the previous raid. But was it possible that he had been left alone for longer, long enough to make his own language? In the weeks before the attack he had used real words. Now, after it, he (or she) began to speak to us. We asked where his family was. He confided that his family were burning in the pits, that His Love was doing it.

'His Love is burning my family. He has to do it.'

'Why?'

'To make them into a new shape.'

The youth had been given no name by Carick. So we decided to call him Alby, and call him a he. On the second day of the storm, Alby was in a small room, screaming.

I had been nominated Father of the House. There was a chance that by having Alby there we were in breach of His Laws, inviting punishment. The screaming sickness made things worse. So I determined that someone should discover whether Alby was male or female, to put an end to the issue and determine if (he) would be allowed to stay or if (she) should be sent away. So two brothers with expertise were sent into the room. When they emerged one of them told me that he would explain to me later in private.

Milk was boiled with seawater and roots. Alby was made to drink it. Moaning and clawing his (or her) stomach, Alby bent and unbent. Saliva poured from the edge of the table to the floor. A muscle in the stomach contracted. Sweat rose up as steam into the room. The head locked backwards and the eyes glazed. They held him or her. Someone said, 'It's coming out,' and I saw the white head of the worm come feeling from the mouth, and the body of the worm slide out in a spasm. One of the two experts was insisting that, in fact, 'all of this was predicted' some years before. A hand grabbed it and the worm was thrown into the fire. It twisted there and contracted. We all sank to our knees and gave words of thanks to His Love.

*

Once, I dreamt a woman was standing before me on a boat. She took me under her cloak and put my face onto her breasts and I said, 'Who are you?' and she said, 'I'm your wife.' I looked over her shoulder and saw a pair of eyes under a hood and I said, 'Who's that?' and she said, 'That's your son.'

Then the boat moved backwards, and I looked down and saw that I was standing on the shore and they were not beside me or even looking in my direction as they floated away.

I went and told someone: 'That's a common dream here,' he said. 'You'll get used to it.'

Another night, I was visited by His Love: a woman came and stood in the room and her eyes had no soul. Instead of a soul was something better, an illumination that flowed out unendingly like a waterfall and seemed to nullify all dangers. She held out a book. On top of the book were a cup and a piece of paper with a picture on it of a face. She put down the book and picked up the cup and poured light out from it onto my feet, as I laughed.

*

On the third day of the storm the earth pounded. A body of smoke like a horn came up from the peak of the mountain on the island to the west: the earth had opened. The smoke became red at the base of the horn. We saw liquid fire jump upwards and outwards in orange gouts which, we knew, would spatter down and start fires, or flow to the black beaches to be hardened by waves. The red, the black and the grey smoke interwove with the ripped-open cover of the clouds. Ashes we knew would fall from the smoke. The rain that would fall on our House would be black.

The rain started. People ran about. Someone chased a goat through a banging door. Men were slipping and scrambling in the mud, slapping their hands over their eyes or their mouths. Alby held onto a rope attached to a canopy, jeering madly at the burning fires in the earth.

Black water ran down the cracks in his face.

I climbed the steps to the ramparts. I looked out to sea. In the distance the cloud had formed a funnel that reached down from the sky and touched the waves. Near the tip of it, the sea flattened and began to spin. There, beyond the edge of the cliff-sides, a whirlpool opened, separate from the storm. Looking into it, I saw the suggestion of bodies, fins or tails that swam with the motion of the water. The core of the pool tightened, and I saw an eye. It was a black eye which flashed into view, scanning the world above it. It was gone, and then it came back. It pivoted and flickered. It was taking in the chaos of the storm. It was almost a casual glance, but precise, the type that a craftsman would give to a thing he had just finished making.

Then it was gone and the pool was erased by the waves.

Dr Jekyll

Yes, I have the respect of the wise and good,
I am wealthy and beloved,
I have made progress and position among
my industrious fellowmen,
but today when I look at them
I am disgusted by their consistent high morals,
their neat hair and clean shirts and waistcoats,
top hats balanced on meek faces.
I hate something familiar about them
  —and then I see it in my cheval glass—
what is familiar in them is me,
my pudgy face, politeness seeping from its pores.
It is me I loathe.
But I have just the tincture for it.
In my dissection room I take
powders from a press in my cabinet;
grinding elements into a compound
with mortar and pestle
I crush that reflection,
place beaker over burner,
lose him in the fog of the ebullient potion,
drink down my remedy,
shrink to my real size,
uncage impatient gaiety, locked up so long
it brims with causeless hatreds and depravity.
To Soho! To fuck prostitutes who wince under
the touch of my corded hairy hands—
their repulsion makes me harder for them.
And when I am done with that
I will beat someone, ecstasy in every blow
I deliver, until I deliver them from life.
Yes, I have the respect of the wise and good,
my industrious fellow men.

Niamh Prior

Freckles

My house is in the woods,
it creaks and listens.

I have my rituals
and an old Transit van.

You could slice the silences here.
Sometimes I go out after dark.

I had a wife once
but she's not coming back.

There is a girl on the checkout,
her name badge says 'Alison'.

Alison has a freckle near her right breast—
there are probably more.

The store closes at ten.
Two cameras watch the car park.

The new set of knives is in the shed
with the ropes. I bought them last week.

Alison had to scan them—one by one.
Her freckle moved with her skin.

I asked if it was real but she didn't answer.
I like freckles.

Times they can be as big as nipples,
times they can come away in your hand.

Gerard Hanberry

To Cure a Body
Lucy Sweeney Byrne

For her ache, she discovered a cure. It was simple, and comparatively pain-free. It worked on a basic principle—that a dull pain is negated by an acute one. To provide an explanation: A person wouldn't mourn athlete's foot, when faced with a sudden, vicious stab wound to the throat. That's the beauty of piercing agony—the pure white sheen that overwhelms the clutter and mud of other, less immediate ills.

Her ache was felt chiefly in the lower stomach. Some referred to it as 'heartache', but for her this was anatomically inaccurate, even absurd. For her, it was located, specifically, in the pit of her womb. (She had not even known before, that she could feel her womb, lurking there inside.) The ache wrapped itself around her fallopian tubes and enveloped her ovaries, making them blueblack-inky-feeling. Her womb's fleshy inner-walls were turned to ash from the grief of it.

To give a sense of the time before the cure: She had developed an odour that she was largely unaware of. It was not dissimilar to that found at the entrance to underground train stations at night in summer—heat and engine oil and sweat and animal and piss and sex rising, with a hint of rose *eau-de-toilette*. Before the cure, her skin had faded pink and grey; vague, hard-to-see colours, blanching meek in between the real ones. She had trouble being. Clawing, gnawing, gnashing—these had been the words for her then.

Before discovering her cure, she had lain awake at night, unable to sleep, because of the dry heat, curling in the corners of her. She hadn't slept for months. Years, even. She'd lain clasping at air and soiled sheets, bunched in fists across the surface of the bed. Her insides had hissed and screeched at her like damp winter logs burning, until she'd felt that she'd sooner go deaf than suffer the sheer endless-wall of it. (Of course though, had anyone been there listening, under the bed or lurking outside the bedroom door, they wouldn't have heard a sound.)

At this time, it would have been a relief for her to end. She couldn't pretend she hadn't dreamt of it; hadn't savoured the taste. She'd imagined it to be like diving head-first into cool waters. Those electric blueberry-jelly waters photographed in catalogues, flicked through idly, while waiting around indoors for nothing in particular on muggy midweek afternoons. She'd imagined ending then to be like a floating outward, in the belly of that water, into nothing, in contact with Nothing. Forgetting the feeling of her body wrapped around her.

But now for a good part: She'd always liked to cook. And to eat! Even more than was necessary. She would have listed insatiability as one of her many defining faults. As a result, in her lingering confinement, she grew fat. A protective thickening of the flesh. Dulling layers swelled across her bones and thoughts. Food fooled her, momentarily, into believing that she was becoming full. Filled. (Similar to the ephemeral satisfaction of another tongue in the mouth, seeking strange, warm spit. Or semen burrowing in, warming the tummy.) Eating afforded her a vague respite, if not yet a cure.

Upon the eve of her discovery, had anyone decided, on a whim, to check in on her, they'd have found her chopping onions by the kitchen sink. The sink faced a window covered in a thin film of grime. The light outside signified day ending. She was making a tomato sauce with Italian sausage and rich egg pasta, and was going to eat it all up with warmed blood-red wine. Soft liquid food to— for a second, maybe—quench the dry ash of her womb. She diced her onions finely, and their odour combined with hers, creating a savoury haze. The slight movements in the atmosphere around her eddied cinders and fumes. The oil was warming in the pan. The radio played, some song about living, and she listened vacantly, through the din of herself.

It was in this absent, ocean-floor state, chopping steadily, that she managed to bring the knife swiftly and expertly down upon the very base of the index finger on her left hand (the one holding the back of the onion in place), severing it from the rest of her body. This was a surprise. Hot ash air escaped her mouth in a sharp rush, only to be sucked in again, quickly, between clenched-jaw teeth. She dropped the knife on the counter top. The sudden clatter was unpleasant. Blood spurted from the twitching finger, and her brand-spanking-new, fingerless stump. The blood felt exposed—it had not expected to be revealed to the world at this moment. It had been coursing happily through hidden tunnels and passageways, murmuring and giggling. Now it came in limp rhythmic waves, an unenthused ejaculate, shamed, the blushing crimson shocking in its vibrancy against the dusky evening light.

The radio played on—another song, something about love, or death. The oil began to emit a faint blue smoke. Impending fire. *Too hot, careful!* She turned off the gas with her remaining five-fingered hand. She paused. The room hung suspended. Blood trickled down her wrist over her elbow, soaking into the cuff of her dress. She knew it must be wet and warm, but she felt—

Nothing

For as long as her memory was willing to unfurl, she'd known her ache. Now, without warning, there was only numbness—that long-sought void. The realisation flitted behind her eyes. But she didn't blink. Her lip didn't even twitch. She was careful not to openly acknowledge, to betray. Not even on the inside of her mind. Someone would see. The ache would see. She knew she needed to conceal the thought from herself, to keep in check this quickening of her heart. To steady now. She breathed through her nose, slowly, deliberately. She waited for the room to settle.

A little aside, a recollection of the world going on around her: At this exact moment, as she stood there, suspended, studying the remaining parts of the hand raised before her face, a cat-shaped blur leaped up onto the windowsill outside, and peered in with yellow orbeyes. It had been attracted from the hedgerow's depths, perhaps by curiosity, or the scent of blood, or perhaps a conscientious awareness of the need, at this point, for a witness. It mewed, feigned a yawn, sleek pink-armoured mouth circling wide, and watched.

Without a word, without even a flicker across her long pinkgrey face, she quickly, asidedly—as though her thoughts were busy elsewhere, on tomorrow's chores maybe, or the tomorrow after's—bandaged up her loss. She used iodine and white porous cloth from the dusty first-aid kit, which sat atop the pine dresser that stood against the beiging wall to the right of the sink. (Note that the shelves of this dresser held no framed photographs, although there was plenty of space for them.)

She took up the knife. She didn't wipe off what had recently been her blood before resuming her dicing. The severed finger, now turning a fashionable off-white—'Severed Digit Pallor'—lay untouched to the left of her onion shards. The browning blood had trickled in a small pool across the grooves of the board, dyeing the layers of onion skin a fleshy pink. Its metallic odour mixed well with the onion's warm wholesome one. She didn't mention to herself what she was doing. The part of her mind in control of doing actions and the part of her mind in charge of taking note of those doings were not in contact with one another just then. She had cut the line. It was easier that way. At this moment, she simply was. A pleasant numb of Nothing. She didn't rush.

She reignited the gas-flame, and tipped onion shards into sizzling virgin oil.

They sloshed and hissed in the pan as she stirred. Their ruddy flavour rose to her nostrils.

The cat-shaped blur watched. It was black, and well-fed, with a red collar and a small silver name tag, but without a bell (for warning birds). The blur sniffed, reaching nose forward, before recoiling, compressing its body back in feigned indifference. It turned its head to the left and squinted closed its eyes.

She added crushed garlic and chopped tomatoes and a little squeeze of lemon, black pepper, salt and a few basil leaves. She added one teaspoon of granulated sugar. And still there was Nothing. The radio—yet another song, something about people and loneliness—continued to evince no reaction from her, although the sounds proved useful for distraction.

But she did realise, deep down somewhere in the quiet places, behind the radio, the hum and sizzle of the ingredients coalescing into soft red in the pot, and her busily clanking mind, that she could hear it, clearly. The absence. There was no screech, no hiss, no groan, no grinding flesh and bone. Anyone who entered her, at that moment, would have found inside only an echoing silence.

The sauce bubbled and reduced and thickened. With surprisingly little difficulty (considering her recent disfigurement), she opened the wine bottle that had been warming by the furnace, and drank deeply from the glass. The tannins slicked the inside of her mouth and throat with blackberries and spice; a thin blood-like film. Her pasta water was simmering and her usual place at the table was set. She lit a long thin white candle with a match, flicking the flame against the box with a sharp twitch of her wrist. Then, the finishing touch: She took out the sweet Italian sausage from the fridge, and smacked the pack onto the bloody chopping board. Her finger lay dead and unburied, slightly to the left. She had not actively remembered nor for one moment forgotten it.

She took her sausages, and cut them lengthways down the middle. She then cut them crossways several times, to create small chunks. She threw the pieces into the bubbling sauce. Next, as though it were just a nothing, not pausing at all in the flow of her motions, she took the finger—cool, like an old man's cheek—and expertly slit it down the middle, from the fingertip to the amputated end. She put down her knife, and neatly removed the chipped nail from its bed, before gently tugging the long thin bone, the small rounded knuckles delicate and white, out from the centre. It came away easier than she'd expected. When she had divided it into two halves, running the silver tip of the blade along with careful precision—it was an elegant finger, she could appreciate that now—she chopped the flesh up crossways into neat little chunks, and, with a swish of the knife, scraped them down off the board and into the pot.

Now, how to convey the following…

It was the greatest meal of her entire life.

It was intoxicating.

When her plate was finished, she piled it up again, and again, until every last scrap was devoured and she'd licked it sparkling clean. Halfway through, insatiable, she opened another red with a pop, arm flung back, and drank straight from the bottle, whacking it down on the table between gulps and smacking her lips together contentedly. She ate with such furious intent that she lost her breath. Sauce spilled down her chin and onto her chest, embedding itself in little caking dollops on her dress and trickling down her décolletage into the rift between her breasts.

She had forgotten a person could feel like this. Her eyes dilated and her body grew supple and soft and willing. Her meat, cooked to perfection, was melting in the mouth. With each bite, she felt stronger. She wanted all of it, thick and red, and she swallowed it all, deep down into her belly. It flooded through her trunk and limbs, heating her from the inside out so that steam rose off her skin, making it glow wet burgundy; like the skins of fat men in saunas. Afterwards, she took the pot into her open lap, legs spread, and ran her remaining fingers around the inside, noisily sucking the last of the sauce off the tips. Her palms and crotch and behind her knees grew sodden. The combined odour emanating from her and her food became overwhelming. The air was dense with the heat and stench of it.

She felt, by the end, like she wanted to tip over the table and set the house on fire and fly screaming naked down the street, eyes ablaze. Sitting there, intoxicated and full at the kitchen table, belly bulging forward, she laughed in the face of her ache. It was really gone, she thought. She laughed, and laughed again, her head back, a guttural rupture booming from the depths of her.

At this point, the story can only provide a sense of things. Of the time after her discovery of the cure: She visited friends. She dined out. She chatted with her mother uninhibitedly, even, occasionally, giggling. She polished the hall mirror, she vacuumed the stairs and behind the couch, and her skin never looked so good. She must have been using new products, they said, because her hair achieved a sleekness previously undreamt of. She bought patterned clothes from high-street shops and pungent, organic cheeses from farmers' markets. She caught the eyes of men who wondered what it might be like to sleep with her, and she smiled coquettishly at them, knowing. She wore purple, and brushed her teeth twice a day, every day. She was so ravishingly engaging, that not one person noticed her missing finger. It was so trivial, a nothing, compared to what she had gained!

She was the embodiment of femininity. Her womb glowed a radiant gold that blinded the women around her and made them secretly jealous. They wondered what her trick was. She was ripe and fresh and fertile, ready for plucking. People said it was a miracle. (Although they'd told her time would do it. They'd told her that time would cure her.)

The respite lasted approximately three months. Without her knowing, a blackblue-inky pearl of history and memory, an embryo too small to be seen by the naked eye, was creating itself from internal whispers almost too quiet for her to hear, and attaching itself, surreptitiously, to the renewed, viscous walls of her womb.

She went to plays by up-and-coming playwrights and tried oysters and laughed at comedy. She read Shakespeare's sonnets on trains, sighing, and had wonderful sex on a picnic rug on a beach with a gentle, cooing poet from Pamplona. But something wasn't right. The pearl was growing, feeding itself on her throwaways, the things she would rather not have known. That comment her sister made; the drunk man at the bar, leering. After a while, her house grew vaguely musty, and she would find herself running out of clean underwear every now and then. There was hair in the shower drain, and she grew uneasy. Once, she awoke in the night, slightly restless. She tripped up in her heels while dancing. She developed cradle cap on her scalp, like a baby, and found herself scratching it on dates with quite charming men, so that the flakes of skin wafted down dreamily into her main courses.

Well. It's easy to guess what had happened. After those three months, she was back where she'd started. No, worse. Her body had developed a bluish-purple rash up her back which itched constantly, leaving blood and matter beneath her nails. Her eyes were sore, and at night, seeped a liquid thicker and milkier than water, which gathered in their inner corners, and which she found smeared across her cheek and pillowcase in the mornings. Her toenails were fraying at the edges, and there were red blotches on her thighs, where hairs refused to surface, burrowing instead back down into her skin. She grew desperate. She needed to be cured again. For longer. She resolved, hands rolled into tight fists (one with five fingers, one with four), to do whatever it took.

Now for the beginning of the end: This time, it took the lower half of her left arm, from the elbow. She made a roast, and feasted on it long into the night. She accompanied the meat with creamed potatoes and delicately steamed carrots and broccoli, dressed in lemon and butter respectively. She flavoured the roast with rosemary and garlic and covered it in generous glugs of oil, to keep it tender. She cooked it at a low heat, for hours. The smell filled the entire street on which she lived, making her neighbours' mouths water with desire. She worked slowly, methodically. This meal was greater even than the last. Tears escaped her, and she laughed, and sighed, and she felt that she understood the expressions artists gave to saints in paintings. This time, the effects lasted a full year. Nobody noticed the missing limb. It was such a minor loss, for so great a gain! Time, they said. Time had healed her.

After the year was out, she barbecued a leg and ate it in the back garden with a bottle of chilled white, and pretty flickering candles to keep the flies away. Later, she made a meatloaf using the tender minced flesh of her breasts.

Her meals kept her going for another four years. She learned to play bridge and developed a fondness for origami. Her father died in the spring of one year and she wore a black dress to the wake. People brought sandwiches of salted cucumber and ham and cheese with the crusts cut off, and told her over drinks that he had been a great man. She changed supermarkets, as she didn't like the customer service at her usual one and thought it was about time she did something about it. She accrued money and bought an opal necklace that was greatly admired by all who saw it, draped around her neck.

Finally, to tell the end—stories like hers must have an end: It was sunny outside, warm. The cat-shaped blur was lounging on the garden table, soaking it in. The cherry tree was blooming, and now and then it snowed down lazy white petals across the lawn. The daffodils were out, grinning and whispering in clusters, and the crocuses too, and small brown birds were flitting to and from the feeder hanging on the kitchen's outer wall. It looked like a picture taken for a classroom with the neatly-written caption, 'SPRING'.

She saw none of this. The pearl of ache had returned, yet again, as she now knew it always would. ('Time', the great healer she'd been promised, seemed to have forsaken her.) She was busy inside, in the shadows, preparing yet again. The curtains were drawn, and from the outside, had anyone been passing, by foot or by car, they'd have thought that perhaps she was away, or had moved somewhere else for a while. Yet there was a stillness to the house that they'd have had trouble describing to others. It would have given them an unnerving sense of anticipation; of potential energy being held, momentarily, in check. The house would have seemed to them somehow disjointed; not fitting with the world marching on around it. Like they'd popped in, quietly, to check on a dozing infant, and discovered a gleaming kitchen knife, resting there alongside it in the cot.

By now, her skin had developed an oily, translucent quality. Her blue veins pulsed limply beneath her cheeks, and along the underside of her remaining wrist. What hair she had left, between the raw blistered patches of scalp, was blanched grey and ratty. It could be found in pungent, damp clusters in dark corners all over the house, and in loose, thin strands across her clothes and bedsheets. Her lips had thinned to nothing, just more skin of face caving in over small stained teeth, with deep creases at each corner. They that had been so full! Her pupils, hard to detect under heavy lids, had become milky and dim. She found it difficult to see from them.

She had placed her bathtub over the fireplace in the living-room, and filled it with water. Now she waited for the water to boil, standing with her silver-topped cane for support. She wore her silk white dressing-gown, already dirtied at the hem. Wedging the top of the cane under the pit of her severed-from-the-elbow left arm, she used her right to drink the wine (dark red, almost black and heavily spiced—a special one, she'd been saving it), and garnish the bathwater with thyme, rosemary, onions and garlic, thickly-chopped carrots and celery, along with anything else appetising she could find in the kitchen presses. (She didn't want anything to go to waste.) There was a drunken recklessness to her movements now, lunging and heavy; to how she threw back the dusty bottle, spilling its contents down her front in staining rivulets; how she lurched from kitchen to living-room, knocking against furniture and doorframes; how she flung in her ingredients, splashing boiling hot water across the carpet, and herself, leaving small steaming red welts on what remained of her skin.

What happened next seems inevitable, barely worth telling. But here it is: When the bath was ready, the room was filled with a hot delicious steam so thick that, standing in the doorway, it would've been almost impossible to see her uneven pinkgrey form emerge from under the dressing gown. If anyone had been there, and called out, to stop her, she wouldn't have heard them anyway. (The ache was screaming in her now.) Anyone present would have only heard, too late, the muffled splash, the sharp intake of breath, as she lowered the last of her body into the boiling stew-water. They'd have been so confused as to what was happening, that there's no way they could have dashed across the thickened, humid room in time to have saved her; to kick the bath from its perch and free her boiled, scorching flesh from cooking any further. They'd never have been able to discern, through the dense white wafts, or beneath the bubbling and swelling red skin, the expression of relief that flitted across her face. But it was there.

And besides—they may not have wanted to admit it to themselves—but had some poor soul been standing there, helpless, in the aftermath, in truth, the most memorable thing about the whole experience—the thing that would have stayed with them for years afterwards, haunting them as they sat at their children's music recitals or dinner party tables or unwrapping gifts on Christmas mornings, the thing that would have filled them with that terrible, heady sensation of desire and shame, a sensation better not acknowledged, as a rule —was, of course, the smell. *That smell!* That delectable, mouth-watering scent, that snaked all across the room, that filled the house, the street, the nearby town, the country, for those lingering minutes, after.

Yes, it's a blessing that nobody was there—whatever people might decide to say now, earnest and frowning, with the corners of their suit-jackets ruckling inward as they lean forward to shake hands; as they smooth hairstyles and flatten out ironed skirts and ties with clean palms, lamenting together in sombre under-voices, with the sickly smell of lilies and roses lacing the air around them.

Really, they should all be relieved. Because, knowing her as they did, they should know now, deep down, had any of them been there with her in those final moments, that this irresistible scent would have overpowered them. It would have forced them—entirely against their will, of course—to make their way over. To glide through the white, swirling room, nose in the air, saliva dripping down their chest, to the remains of her: so hot and flavoured and naked and willing. The scent—and their desire—would have grown richer, more overwhelming by the foot-thud, filling their nose, suffocating their mind, as they approached. Finally, it would have impelled them, once they stood by her side, to reach down. To touch, and gently pull away—so ready, the soft, yielding, hairless flesh, easing into their moist fingers—one last piece. To take just one inevitable bite of her.

And so it is probably for the best, that not one of those who knew her were with her for the last portion of her cure. Fortuitous, really, that she was entirely alone. By the time anyone thought to look, there was Nothing left to find. Nothing, but a few white bones cloaked in dust, a full-bellied, cat-shaped blur on the sill of the open window, preening itself with its coarse, thrusting tongue, and that final, restful silence.

Gums

Remember that night, my love, when
your teeth fell out, one by one,
your yellowed pearls patting the carpet like rain
and you let them lie,
hardly looking.
                            I swept them away.

The first day it seemed amusing,
a joke to tell the office about.
'Lo!—what misfortune you had!'
It could only have happened to you
(or potentially your dad, he's very like you)
but by the second day it seemed
less spry. Your eye-teeth were gone
and you could only gouge morsels
from marshmallows and curly fries.

By day five you were gummy, old; lips
flayed back over moony-boned sockets.
You couldn't keep your tongue inside,
it lolled and looked at me with
curious eyes.
Your grin was outrageous, horrendous,
and then your own eyes were gone,
rolled back under those widening lips, fat rubber tides;
as your tongue—a skullcapped slug—protruded
from within, smoothly slipping
from your thin discarded skin.

I turned away from you, ran like mad.
I'm afraid you're still entombed there,
inside the slug, drugged,
or maybe you've been a beast all this time
and the growing old together
has revealed illusory skin turned loose; falling away
like dampened paper.

The mirror shows my own skin, thinned
through the years like Miss Havisham's veil.
Under fingers, I am dried and clotted mud,
mouth resolutely closed, tongue touching gums.

Caroline Hardaker

The ghost was not a normal one

so I let it in.   It didn't wail nor rattle chains
nor hoard *boos* within its throat.

Its clothes were form-fitting,
& it was fond of toast   but had an aversion to jelly,

explaining it was on a diet.   We spent hours
watching sports together,

mostly hurling & archery,
& when I turned on a scary movie,   it fled the room.

Our conversations were wide-ranged   but boring,
never broaching subjects

such as death, as I feared
I might easily offend it.   I never asked for its name

but sensed I was privileged   & considered it a friend.
I felt I was one step away

from entering the loony bin;
but my friend had it worse,   its two feet in the grave.

After a while,   I discovered its name was Harold
& that it—*he*—was fond of my dog.

To rehearse my own death,
I shadowed his movements,   taking cues

from how he reacted   to everyday happenings;
but after several weeks,

I realised he wasn't a ghost:
He was a person as lonely as I'd been   but not as gullible.

Then, one day,   he left me with my solitary thoughts
& took my dog along with him.

Jonathan Greenhause

Re-Animator Tales
Ronan Flaherty

During the 1800s, Giovanni Aldini, Professor of Physics at the University of Bologna, applied electrical current to the severed heads of executed criminals, producing spasmodic movement from facial muscle that gave the appearance of life returning to these bodiless heads. Aldini conducted his experiments in front of select audiences. Austrian counts, bejewelled *grande dames*, Milanese financiers, wives and mistresses dressed in summertime muslin, overindulged young noblemen sporting the then fashionable Bedford crop, men of science, all would sit in short well-ordered rows in large dimly-lit rooms and wait for the show to begin.

History wants great men to be great but also trussed with a fringe of wrongdoing. Nature, we know, is rounded by its imperfection.

~

Caffeinated and careworn, we both overuse internet search engines. We view funny/unfunny videos on YouTube. We binge watch on Netflix. We ignore emails. We pass time.

The white summer dress patterned with cockatiels is an old one, you tell me, from when you lived in Brighton and owned the second-hand pushbike with the mint-green frame. File folders on the hard drive of an old laptop, filled with party photos of bleary-eyed friends whose names are rarely recalled.

'That's Jean.' 'Elaine's there on the right with the long blonde hair.' 'That's Lucy, Jean's friend.' 'Elaine, she's the one who has the Betty Boop tattoo.'

You maintain that when the possibility of reinvention exists, cannot every life start anew?

~

On a December morning in 1802, George Forster, an out of work coachmaker, waits for his wife by a lock gate at Paddington Canal. A mutual friend has arranged the meeting between the estranged young couple. Recent snowfall lightly dapples the embankment. The surface of the canal is scabbed-over in places with glassy crusts of ice, dank water underneath. Forster huffs on his purpling hands, shuffles his feet. His wife will be bringing along their infant daughter while their two older children remain in the workhouse up in Barnet. He knows she will ask for money, those few coppers amongst the lint in his coat pocket. Above all, she will demand from him that they become a family again. He will tell her he plans to remove his children from the workhouse that very afternoon, forever shot of bone meal and colicky coughs. The money in his pocket will buy them dinner. They will be a family again.

~

You obsessed over a dead young woman, a traffic victim, immortalised by a corroded bicycle frame attached to a railing opposite a busy intersection in south-east London. The weather-bleached photograph attached to the handlebars showed her smiling against an empty horizon. The same age as my sister, you said.

~

Giovanni Aldini had, with his Roman Emperor curls, bow-tied silk cravat and frockcoat of bistre black, created with an impresario's dash what for the Age of Enlightenment must have appeared the ultimate parlour trick.

~

There was the story we followed through online news sites about a young couple convicted of a scam at a British airport that involved the claiming of lost and unclaimed luggage. The girlfriend had become fascinated by the clothing and personal effects she found within this misplaced baggage and the lives they suggested. She took to wearing wigs along with the stolen clothes and created multiple identities. The scheme had been exposed when her boyfriend had assaulted her and she had charges pressed against him. We debated what might have happened. Maybe the swindle was not bringing in the fortune he thought it would and this had him take his frustrations out on the girl. Perhaps he suspected that the girlfriend, who he would send to reclaim the luggage, was hiding the valuables. He might have also felt that in pursuing these alternative existences she was on some level being unfaithful to him. Then again, you said, he might just have been a sociopath. Either way, she went to the police.

~

In the parlour room of a neoclassical villa, a small gathering is seated on satin-covered Regency chairs. Attention has focused at the top of the room, where a man in a frockcoat approaches a suspended human head. Opposite the head stands a small metal column consisting of discs of zinc and copper interspaced with conductive layers of cloth. The man in the frockcoat produces a set of metal tongs which he applies to the face of the severed head. No one speaks. By today's standards the pyrotechnics are minimal. There are no pale blue dancing Tesla-coil tendrils of electricity, no rasps of static. Instead, sudden gasps resonate from the onlookers as the face of the executed criminal begins to twitch. The corners of the mouth spasm in elastic movement and the cheeks undulate. Breaths grow deeper among the small audience. Then the eyelids flicker, as if about to wake from a long slumber. The re-animated face breaks into a grimaced smirk, before relaxing back into a dead man's frown. Silence settles once more in the room.

~

There was the laptop that lasted until the plastic hinges cracked like fissured skin, the screen buckled and the pixels died in large cloud-shaped patterns. Then there is the tablet down the side of our bed with the fractured display. You invoke cases of lead poisoning in cities in China and in areas of West Africa, cesspits filled with circuit boards, discarded mobile phones piled as high as termite mounds. Copper nodes and wiring pried like gold from long dead teeth.

~

Aldini was a nephew of Luigi Galvani, the Italian anatomist who applied electrical current to the legs of dead frogs by means of two separate conductors, one made of copper and one made of zinc. Galvani's experiments demonstrated how electrical current is involved in the process of life.

Count Alessandro Volta, the inventor of the world's first battery, the Voltaic pile, after whom the unit of electromotive force was named, confined his experimentation to sheets of paper.

~

More conscious now, we avoid websites with prominent cookie warnings and no longer download third-party modifications for our apps. We learn how to defrag and perform system restore. We share your old laptop between us. We do not buy the newly released iPhone model. A more important decision has still to be made. We have reached an impasse. There are, you tell me, other females, whose skin gleams like the models from shampoo commercials. Then there was Alex from your job, who told you how stars scintillate rather than twinkle and how so much wonder is missed through our common misapprehensions.

Later, he explained how death is the permanent termination of consciousness, the end of our individuality, a thought so horrible many cling to the notion of an afterlife.

You started meeting him after work. It was because he listened.

You would still text him, even after…

Why do we wait, you say, when we are faced day-in with the reality of our transitory nature? Can we throw our old selves out with our old phones?

~

You receive an email from a college friend who has not contacted you in over four years. The subject line of the email reads: **eaRn CA$$$h from home N0w!!!!**

~

Mary Shelley, author of *Frankenstein*, in writing her famous novel about human flesh re-animated, had supposedly been influenced by tales of Giovanni Aldini and his experiments.

~

I know how the news, with its distillation of death and destruction, depresses you. Often I find myself ignoring the newsreader and instead paying close attention to the headlines scrolling across the bottom bar. In the ether, victim and perpetrator now attain some level of immortality.

Yesterday's news waits to be searched. The past has come to be inescapable.

~

In January 1803, Aldini would travel to England, and Newgate Prison, in order to attain a complete corpse on which to experiment. The body—procured, some say, with the blessing of a sympathetic magistrate—was to be that of a recently executed man named George Forster, an unemployed coachmaker, hung for supposedly drowning his wife and their infant daughter in Paddington Canal. Despite a confession, many friends and acquaintances believed Forster innocent of the crime.

~

We had argued. I told you I disliked Alex, his glib logic and soft knowing smile. You were quick to inform me Alex was not arrogant, merely self-assured. I countered this. 'Fuck him, what does he know.' You then did that thing with your eyes, also that other thing you do when you skim your top teeth over your lower lip. You folded your arms and looked away.

Within weeks this disagreement about Alex seemed like a prelude to what happened to him, an invocation of the Fates.

~

As a convicted murderer, George Forster would have known his mortal remains were destined for medical dissection. On the night before his execution, Forster tried to kill himself in his cell with a crudely fashioned blade. This type of suicide was not uncommon at the time. With a quick death on the scaffold far from guaranteed, more than a few condemned would view taking their own life on the eve of their execution as the ultimate assurance against the failure of the hangman's noose, lest they suffer a slow strangulation, or come to while under the surgeon's scalpel and endure a vivisection.

~

I return one afternoon to find you have stickered over the laptop's webcam, that ogling spyhole which you have begun to regard with suspicion.

Thereafter you delete all your virtual accounts, even your email addresses.

~

The experiment that took place in the Royal College of Surgeons (recorded for posterity in *The Newgate Calendar*) was unsuccessful. Surrounded by a small group of spectators, Aldini applied electrical current to various parts of Forster's body. Facial muscle writhed and limbs were set aquiver. A dead eye was seen to open, a fist clenched as if grasping for the very air itself.

George Forster did not return to life.

Unsuccessful in his attempt to surpass his previous experiments, Aldini returned to the Continent lamenting his failure. This contemporary of Galvani and Volta, notwithstanding the fortune and esteem he earned, never achieved the greatness he judged within his reach.

~

You leave Alex's number in the contacts list on your mobile phone for seven months. When at last you press delete, you are struck by the finality of it. 'I can't believe he's gone,' you say.

Someone leaves your life for good, but still remains in the same room, the same bed.

That invisible world said to be home to unseen currents and unheard frequencies conceivably represents that invisible space between life and death. This, you say, will be the place where we survive.

Forrester
Trevor Fevin

Forrester was weird. That was my first impression. He said he couldn't talk about his job, it was something hush hush. No, actually he didn't use those words, I inferred them, but I suspected it was Intelligence work. The day he moved in, a security guy turned up to fit a scrambler to our phone and returned frequently to sweep the apartment for buggings. Forrester would only say that it was 'necessary' for his work. There was the zoo smell when he left his door open, and those odd grunts and yelps in the night, which might have been down to bad dreams or solo sex jinks. And then, in the shower, I began finding what appeared to be scales, the same size and colour as lime-pastel honesty seeds. I contemplated boxing them up and sending them to the Zoological Society with a simple query like, 'What sort of reptile is this?'

He paid his rent, at least, which I depended on (this is London), and seemed comfortably off, whatever it was he did. Expensive suits, nice stuff I admired, and good shirts, double-cuffed with diamond links; a signet ring on his left little finger, lumpy gold with a diamond dint. But didn't Intelligence operatives need to be 'grey men', unlike Forrester? He was always the first man you'd notice in a crowd, tall and bigly built. Most of his head seemed concentrated in meaty jaws, like a Rottweiler, belittling his eyes to small and squinty nicks of piercing blue.

I never saw him date anyone, neither boy nor girl. He ate breakfast with me, *tête-a-tête*, which was nice, but he appeared to consume only meat. Huge amounts passed through the refrigerator: steaks, plaited chitterlings, purplish kidneys, piled spirals of red fatty grindings. For many weeks, he kept almost entirely to his room, and I had little more than glimpses of him, listening on headphones, or occasionally plinking at an electronic keyboard.

I had a guinea pig and I loved it, petted it until it purred. It was all I could have, no dogs or cats allowed by the lease. It went missing. I suspected Forrester right away. You would, after all that meat in the diet. And my instincts were telling me. I questioned him. 'Sorry mate,' was his reply. 'No idea. Probably ran away. I expect they do that.'

The middle of one night, Forrester came into my room, naked and ready for anything. It was after the guinea pig mystery. I, myself, can be receptive to a lot of things like this, I mean, someone making advances. It all depends. But it was a shock to discover Forrester wanted me that way. I said no, no, but he did it anyway, brutal and nasty. He went in for biting, and sweated an animal stink.

First my pet, then me.

Something had to change. A locksmith came and fitted a lock and bolts to my bedroom door. I purchased a rape alarm, slipped a note under Forrester's door. *Please get out of my apartment*, which he ignored. A few days later there was a reply under my door. *This place suits me, and so do you. I thought you wanted what happened. There'll be no repeat, promise. Amaury xx.*

Those bloody kisses. *Wanted* it?

After that, I avoided him in the kitchen, and he stopped breakfasting or watching TV with me. I've got to be honest, I felt it, like a tooth missing after the dentist has pulled it. But I was thinking *rape* all the time, like when you can't help chewing on words like *beheading* and *cancer*, and I began stopping out a lot at cinemas and shops, walking stores from end to end and drinking at cocktail bars and nightclubs, all places I'd never normally frequent. All to avoid Forrester. That's when I met Breda.

My first impression was she was dithersome, like a drag act. She was all over me from the off, and I soon decided she would do for now, and moved her in. I wasn't in love with her, it wasn't necessary, and I don't think she cared two hoots for me, either. With Breda, it was sex at first, then money. As for me, I needed to know I could still hack it with a woman after Forrester. And I could, but the thing had shifted. Truth was, I liked it better with Forrester.

My bedroom became Breda's dressing room. My clothes were mostly routed from the wardrobe for space to house her expensive frills and fusses, the fake furs and strapless skimps. Many nights, the wardrobe doors burst open with a crack from the pressure of all her ruched attire. Unguents and essences populated the dressing-table. I couldn't find my hair gel or brush any longer. Shoes were paired everywhere, under the bed, on the windowsill, and a rank Parisian stink engulfed us nightly, fugging the air like powdered asbestos. 'Did you spray the actual bed?' I asked one day, but she didn't answer. She rarely answered, once she was moved in.

It wasn't long before she had got someone to remove the lock and bolts from our bedroom. 'We don't want to seem unfriendly,' she said. 'Besides—I feel trapped, locked in with you every night.' I guessed what she was chasing. Hard luck for her, though, because Forrester didn't like her. There were a few spats in the kitchen. He hissed at her, and one morning tried to bite her. Breda screamed murder, and a couple of mugs got smashed.

'What are you going to do about it?' she snarled at me. 'He needs to be told.'

By then, I had no need to think it over. '*You* should move out,' I said. 'That's the best solution.'

'I've got no money,' she said. 'All my cards are maxed. Sub me, and I'll go.'

So I made a substantial donation to be rid of her, including the cost of taxiing all her baggage to the new billet.

'Well, she was a bad idea,' Forrester said. We had soon resumed our breakfasts *à deux*. 'By the way, I'm sorry about the guinea pig.'

'You bastard.'

He was microwaving bacon, sausages, black pudding with its mystery pearly bits (what is that stuff?). There was a steamy carnal odour, and the sound of Forrester eating mouthily, open-wide style. 'We don't need anyone else around here, you and me,' he said. 'And don't look at me like that.'

'I know what you are,' I said. 'You don't fool me.' I tried to swallow. 'You're not even human. I know you can change shape. Your face alters, and I've seen the weird lights coming from your room. Why don't you show me your real body? Go on.' I hadn't meant to say that much. Until then, it had only been suspicion in my mind.

'Best not, mate. You don't want that. It'll scare the shite out of you. Let's just say, I can do human, I can do nice, whatever you want. I can love people— love you. I'll try much, much harder. Only, be warned. I've got my limits, short temper and stuff. And don't be stupid around me. I don't suffer fools.' He had eaten all his breakfast and was wiping the last traces of grease and blood off the plate with his fingers and licking it off. Abruptly he stopped; stood behind me, gripped me in his arms and briefly jammed his head—*clunk*—against mine. His goodbye kiss was like a dart landing on my neck. Beneath the aftershave came an elusive funk of pond-weed, something foetid. I brushed against tightly-bunched muscles under his shirt, pale and luminous in the cold morning light.

We slept together every night after this, and I forgave the guinea pig thing. Sex is sex, after all, it's what you want, and I'd come around, though there were drawbacks, particularly when the reptile under the skin peeped out. The fact is, Forrester's hologram, or whatever trick it was, did occasionally slip. And there were those stinks; the raw meat diet; the eyes shifting to acid green slits. Believe me, glittering reptilian eyes in the bedroom's half-light, looking me up and down like I was dinner, were not nice. Those times when he was annoyed, he hissed like a steam-hammer and his teeth morphed into needles. I kept a good distance, then.

I was soon into the routine of being with him, acceptant, and falling in love. Yes, I know, don't bother lecturing me. You can't love someone who terrifies you. Only he did, and I did, and there it is. We breakfasted and dined together, and weekends, there were marathons of greedy sex, leaving me cracked, battered, blissy. I gave up girlfriend-hunting, forgot about women entirely and we began travelling together. He told me a few things: his mother was French, his father a criminal doing a long stretch for something really bad (unspecified—I suspected murder). He had, he said, found it 'complicated', coming to terms with what he was, took comfort that he wasn't alone in having this weird genetic inheritance. 'You'll find us everywhere in public life,' he said. 'Just look—politicians, big showbiz names.' He named some well-known people. Some of it—his appetites—he battled with. I wondered about cannibalism, but there might have been even worse proclivities, things I didn't want to name. He never actually said MI6, but I was sure it was where he reported, day in, day out. He talked non-committally of the world of Intelligence—nowadays, he said, it focused on gas and oil supplies, the people one bought them from, and the delicate balance of international relations. It was dangerously complex, dealing with Russians, Saudis, the Chinese. Any operative had to have a precise comprehension of consequences.

'Just look at Libya,' he said. 'Look what we did to Iraq.'

I said I knew nothing of international politics. 'Always vote Labour and leave it at that.' He snorted at me. 'I thought you had more sense.' Yes, Forrester was more intelligent than me. He had, after all, masterminded his way to Oxford, then Harvard—where, I suspect, he'd first been recruited by some agency or other. He hinted at grotesque players I knew I'd never choose to meet. 'You live in an Enid Blyton world,' he said. 'No clue what's out there. It's not like that for me. Oh, by the way, I'm being sent abroad soon. I may be gone as long as a year, I don't know yet.'

This hit me in the guts. I'd never loved before, and now this. 'I won't be able to contact you,' he said. 'No calls or emails. The office won't tell you anything, either.' So matter-of-fact about it, he was, like a man under sentence.

'What office? What do they know about me?'

'Well—everything. They have to.'

He was going somewhere in the Middle East—probably—but couldn't give details. Later, before leaving, he admitted it was a high-risk mission, every mission was. I could find no comfort anywhere. I pictured him captured, imprisoned, tortured. Probably some ghastly execution, beheading most likely. I saw little chance of getting him back alive and unmaimed.

My last snapshot of him: passport on the kitchen worktop, suitcase packed (he travelled questionably light) and him, wearing uncharacteristic casuals—pale summery slacks and polo shirt, luminously marked kickers, sunglasses wedged in his buzz-cut. We had our final hug, his bruising kiss (he couldn't do any other kind). And he was gone.

Months passed; a whole year, as he had predicted. Towards the end of that time there was a postcard, from Riyadh. *My last voyage. After this, I'm yours*, it said. Unsigned, of course.

A full fifteen months after leaving, he stumbled through my door. I had waited, could do no different, and he was back and, I saw at once, dying. His skin was the grey of stone, his breathing terrible. I helped him into bed. 'They poisoned me,' he said, 'I don't know what they used, but it's probably hopeless. Get an ambulance anyway.' Reptile eyes glowered often, as the hologram slipped—it happened a lot then—and I had to jump clear when the alligatorish head darted at me. I didn't ask who poisoned him. Maybe I didn't want the responsibility of knowing. Before the ambulance could collect him, there was an interception: men in white overalls swarmed in, taking us both by plain van to a private ward, complete with armed guard. They let me stay with him and we clung together, for days it seemed, as he wrestled against death.

He pulled through, but my arm is gone. It was the left one, torn off by those needle teeth during the worst of his frenzies. I had to leave him then, for emergency treatment, transfusions and stitches. Nothing could be done to save the arm because it was gone, inside of him. I have forgiven him, of course. We were bludgeoning fate to save him and I guess a sacrifice was called for. When he was in his right mind again, he asked, 'What happened to your arm?' I hesitated, still too traumatised, and then he said, 'Oh. I see.'

There are debriefings now. People coming and going. I make tea, keep out of the way. I am tormented by phantom limb pains, off and on.

A file exists, he says, notes on a new mission. Phrases like *prolonged fieldwork* and *ultra-sensitive* slip from his lips. I see his need, greedy for fresh testing. And one raw look—junglyand bleak—tells me our future, even as he reaches for the hand that is still mine.

Bogeyman

1st March 1965

When I was one they resurrected him,
dug up the scraps of bone from Pentonville quicklime,
packed them in oak, draped flags, slow-marched
the gun-carriage through sleety 60s streets.

Snow flickered images on our TV screens,
huddled crowds signing as the carriage crossed
to the beat of Charles Mitchell's sonorous tones
requiem in pacem.

Did it come from this, that first terror?
Did I confuse Casement with the Michan's Mummy,
think his Glasnevin tomb must be visited,
a crusty hand shaken?

Was it he who made shadows darken
on the landing, exert a gravitational pull
through the door of the upstairs bedroom,
towards the wardrobe where the bogeyman hid

till displaced by whatever fear *du jour*
gripped me more bonily?
In the 70s it was 'Tubular Bells'
that lowered temperatures, raised sheets.

In the 80s it was whatever blood carried
in illicit veins through dangerous apertures.
Each decade found its own swirling vortex
of imps straddling chests, white mares snorting.

It ends with the banality of a waiting room:
a dead celebrity waving from the cover of an old *Hello*,
a raised bump beneath skin, a white-draped man
scanning penumbras on illuminated screens.

Nessa O'Mahony

Essay | Dead Baby v Dead Baby:
The Power of Humanity in Creating *Penny Dreadful*'s Horror
Rachel Sneyd

To the best of my recollection there are only two dead babies in *Penny Dreadful*. I say 'only' because, well, it's *Penny Dreadful*—a show where De Sade's brutalised sex slave, Justine, baptises herself in the blood of her freshly murdered abuser before engaging in a threesome with Dorian Gray and the Bride of Frankenstein. Over the top is writer/creator John Logan's baseline, and he delights in breaking taboos in order to shock and provoke us. Other ostensibly dark and violent shows might shy away from infant death, but not *Penny Dreadful*. It's the contrast between the ways that these two babies' deaths are presented and not simply the show's willingness to 'go there', however, that really offers us an insight into the nature of horror.

The first dead baby is snatched on a train by an apprentice witch. It's carried back to a gothic mansion in a handsome leather bag, and then the head witch cuts out its heart and sews it into a voodoo doll. She chats away to the Devil as she works, and the heart starts to beat. Just before we cut to the episode's credits she leans in and kisses the doll. Sensuously. The sequence is creepy as hell, and made me squirm in my chair and watch through my fingers. It didn't frighten me, though. Season Two's principal antagonist orders families slaughtered and mutilates her victims' corpses because of course she does: she's the villain. *Penny Dreadful* has no shortage of monsters in its villains and anti-heroes—some recognisable from the horror canon, others Logan's originals. All of them sharing a universe is the premise the show is built on, but the gore they generate is stylised and sensationalised to the degree that it often shocks without penetrating deeper—into either the viewer's sensibility or the nature of horror itself.

There's a surreal quality to the experience of binge-watching that really suits this show. I watched all twenty-seven episodes in a week and a half, fuelled by coffee and a need to see if the writers would ever find a storyline bizarre enough to best Eva Green's acting talents (not even close). As the episodes blurred together I found myself seeing beyond the messy, occasionally half-hearted season arcs and realising that the show's surface narrative is a means to an end. The real point is the search for humanity that happens between the big plot points. Our damaged anti-heroes are circling each other warily, desperate to feel human and have their humanity recognised. Every once in a while they collide in just the right way, and the results are glorious.

An impromptu dance lesson between a social outcast and an empathetic stranger.

A potentially embarrassing shopping trip where a woman expertly teases her inexperienced friend without ever humiliating him.

One guarded immigrant helping another to wash the dishes after tea.

These small moments, achingly simple and honest, are what gives the show its true power. Forget finding 'dear Mina'—Bram Stoker's heroine transformed into a beautiful blonde innocent whose kidnapping motivates her guilt-stricken childhood friend, Vanessa, to enter the demon-hunting business—and forget defeating the Devil-Dracula fraternal tag-team. What really drives these characters, whether they're self-aware enough to recognise it or not, is the desire for human connection. And, of course, the fear of it. Star-crossed should-be-lovers Vanessa and Ethan might tell us they're afraid of unleashing the literal evil inside themselves, but the disillusioned American frontiersman doesn't walk away from Green's gorgeously, gloriously fractured Vanessa and her plea to build a life together because of his feral shadow-self. Not really.

One of the many odd, little lessons that depression's taught me is that the worst part isn't the bit where you're down in the hole. Obviously that bit is bad. It's awful. But you're kind of numb at that point. All the awfulness becomes fuzzy and meaningless. It's when you're coming out from all that, after you've clawed your way back up towards normal, that you have to feel the fear and the shame and the full-on despair. We all ache to escape the darkness, but to have felt pain is to fear the light.

Which brings us to the mother of the second dead baby. Lily.

Oh, Jesus, Lily.

In the first season, Billy Piper's Brona / Lily is a tragic Irish prostitute, eking out a living on London's edge, while consumption slowly kills her from within. Her accent's dodgy, but her laugh rings true. She's tough, sincere, and painfully—verging on trope-ily—alive. Of course Ethan falls in love with her. And, of course, emotionally stunted man/boy-of-science Victor Frankenstein chooses her: first as slab of woman-shaped meat to shock back to life and present to his

Creature as a bride, later as his own perfect, sweetly simple zombie lover. And then the show throws us its one great twist. Lily overpowers the Creature when he tries to force himself on her, and we realise that she's self-aware. Unlike Ethan and Vanessa, Lily has no intention of hiding in the hole. She's mad as hell, and finally we're face to face with a character who isn't afraid to feel. A character who demands her pain and chooses to let it define her.

The more Lily tells us she's a monster, the more we see the woman. Fierce. Refusing to bend to the men who desperately try to shape her: Victor and the Creature, who claim they want to love her, but only see the outline of her—a pretty girl without the blood and guts and scars. And Dorian, who only desires her as a playmate so long as she keeps having the right kind of fun, so he can live vicariously through her. Comment sections under reviews of *Penny Dreadful* are stuffed full of questions about Dorian's relevance. 'Why is he in the show?' 'Yeah, he's hot, but does he do anything except have sex?' 'Is his storyline ever going to impact anyone else?' It wasn't until I watched the Season Three finale, after Dorian betrays Lily and surrenders her to Frankenstein and his twisted medical-school frenemy Henry Jekyll (ingeniously imaged by Logan as an Indo-Scot with a colony-sized chip on his shoulder), that I fully understood the character's role myself. Dorian represents the consequence of the loss of humanity in a person. All the emptiness of his narrative, reflected in the visual glitz that surrounds his every scene—the opulent but sterile mansion, the glamorous but pointless balls, the classical music sounding just so slightly off as it blares from his gramophone—suddenly made perfect sense.

But if Dorian doesn't feel, if there's not enough of the man left inside him for that, does his betrayal of Lily really sting? Is it really so awful? Not particularly, I'd argue. No more than Dracula tricking Vanessa, or the witch sacrificing the baby. He's just another monster obeying his nature. To be truly cruel you have to have the capacity for empathy. It's the purposeful base hurts that ordinary people inflict on each other that are the most horrific. The ice-cold betrayal of Vanessa's mentor, the Cut Witch, and Ethan attacking the Indian village while serving in the US army. Whatever the hell it was that Mina's father/Vanessa's father figure, the daring adventurer Sir Malcolm, did to the unfortunate people living on the lands he 'discovered' in Africa. These are the dark secrets in our Scooby Gang's pasts, the origin stories that formed them into the literal (and metaphorical) monsters that they are today. For me personally, it's Victor's decision to enlist Dorian in capturing and neutering Lily that's the most viscerally disturbing choice in the show, because we've seen the goodness in him. We know Victor well enough to know that he knows better, and we know what the consequences of such a sin could be upon his soul.

Which, finally, brings us to that second dead baby. The one that really gets under your skin.

This time it's a death that happens off-screen. We've previously seen a simple shot of a grave, instead of the freakily life-like rubber dummy that the witch carved up. Now, finally, trapped in Jekyll's laboratory, Lily narrates her origin story to Victor, and we look her right in the eye as she tells it. A tale of poverty and the isolation of a fallen woman. Compounded by a hard winter and a harder man. The kind of small tragedy that happened over and over in Victorian London, and ever before, and ever after. Baby Sarah's death didn't end the world, or save it. No one mourned her but her mother. But that doesn't mean her death didn't matter. Lily has no care for ego anymore, no fear of the depths inside herself. And so she begs Victor not to steal the memory of her daughter away from her.

Victor slowly approaching a shackled, broken Lily with a syringe of bad-thought-erasing serum is the most truly frightening moment of *Penny Dreadful*. I was sick to my stomach watching it. I was crying. Victor isn't evil, or a minion in the thrall of evil. He's an arrogant, self-centred boy who's about to make a choice that will shape the course of someone else's life, and that he will have to live with for the rest of his. How blood-chillingly monstrous is it for him to hold this power over her, and how appropriate that Lily's last hope is an appeal to his humanity. 'There are some wounds that never heal. There are scars that make us who we are. But without them, we wouldn't exist.' This is the knowledge Lily had carried back with her when she clawed her way up from the depths of despair, a lesson I had to learn for myself in order to stop fearing the person that depression transformed me into.

It's all well and good for Logan to shock us with a grotesque image of a dead baby, but there's always another creator willing to push our collective tolerance for gore even further. *Penny Dreadful*'s most meaningful contribution to the genre, and to the fraught question of the nature of horror itself, lies in what it evokes through Baby Sarah's mere memory—our helplessness in the face of fate's cruel twists, the inevitable cost of loving other mortals, and our bottomless capacity to inflict pain.

conditions from diabetes to cancer and a wide range of cardio-vascular diseases would seem to be ample motivation to me.

VOICE ONE:

And now to the results of this study, Sara – it has taken close to two years for their public dissemination. What are your reactions to this delay, from an ethical point of view?

VOICE THREE:

Well, of course, in Great Britain we are accustomed to our universities receiving subsidies from government to fund research and student places – although increasingly less following the Government Education Act of 2022. R'lyeh University, however, is an entirely privately-funded research institute located in Switzerland. They are not legally obligated to share any data obtained in research studies that they and the consortium financed and to which participants had signed up to, having agreed to these conditions. Legalities are one thing – however, ethically this takes us into quite a different terrain. A reasonable delay caused by checking results, interpreting data, ensuring no results were doctored and no anomalies included in the data set is to be expected. But *two years* [speaker's emphasis] before sharing pioneering data that is expected to revolutionise treatment methods and utterly alter patient prognoses appears, to some, to be indicative of a research project in which the ethos has been to leave one's humanity at the threshold.

VOICE ONE:

And have you any thoughts as to reasons for this delay, Sara? What possible benefit could there be to the team at R'lyeh in postponing publication of their results?

VOICE THREE:

One line of thought might suggest profitability – a confidential trade agreement with a multi-national pharmaceutical company, giving them a two-year head start on developing patented microsphere technology. Another reason could be that the microsphere project is just the tip of the iceberg, a front for a much more extensive project, the existence of which R'lyeh denies and the nature of which can only be speculated. The microsphere study may be, according to this line of thought, a red herring from the main

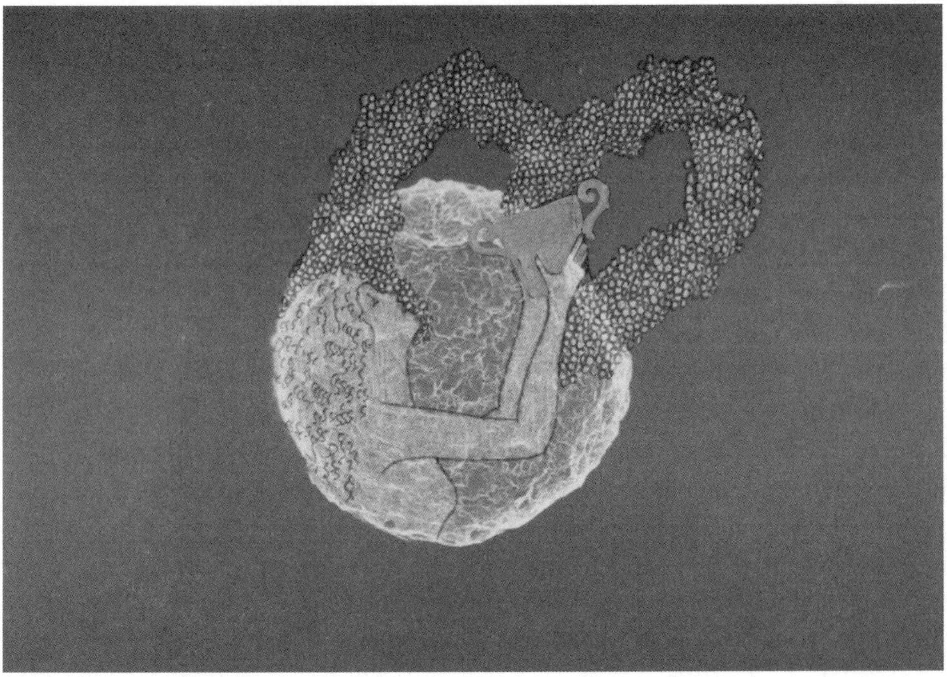

The Guinea Fowl
Olivia Heal

Once upon a time a woman gave birth to a bird.
Neither mother nor midwife batted an eyelid: the birth was straightforward, the bird-child had the creased pink skin of any other bantling.
The woman raised it as one of her own, despite the wing stumps in place of arms, the claws where there should have been toes.
When it was two months old the bird became covered in white fluff.
When it was six months old the bird sprouted feathers, these grew to be grey-black chiffon feathers, specked with white dots.
The bird was a guinea fowl.
Only at this point did the woman's husband acknowledge the child's abnormality.
He accused his wife of participating in coitus with a bird.
Outraged that an avian rival usurp his position, he killed the bird-offspring.
He wrung its neck, plucked it still warm and hung it for a week above the front door that no other male challenge his virility.
For these seven days the woman wore black and did not speak.
On day seven he eviscerated the bird, made a stock of its neck, heart and gizzard.
The woman cursed her doubting husband with all her might.
He stuffed the bird with its own liver and roasted it in its own juices.
The smell of pot roast guinea fowl filled the house, causing the woman to flee.
He fed the braised bird to his five other non-bird children.

Elsewhere a guinea fowl hen hatched out an infant.
She raised the infant as one of her own.
The child lives with the birds to this day. Naked. Featherless. At dusk, the child-bird crows like a guinea fowl.

The Trade

Magic happens here. My rooms are filled
with spells for love, for lust,
for health, for wealth, and they deliver—
I have the testimonials.

The cost is merely losing all
one's health, or wealth, or love, or lust,
and isn't due until a year has passed.
My customers are sure the choice

will not be difficult, and a year
is very long, and anyway
I'm much too small to enforce the deal,
they think. They change the subject,

ask me if I use spells on myself.
I don't tell them that my happiness
comes from not desiring what I haven't got,
not wishing that the calendar would stop,

and not imagining their eyes, when the time
is up, and they must give away
what once seemed so easy to choose.
Nobody buys from me twice.

But there's always someone new
who'll make the trade, not noticing
the cold here, or my assistant
in the shadows, counting down the days.

Alex Harper

Real Boys
Clara Kumagai

Before I was a donkey, I was a boy.

I've been in this same field for a while now. It might be years. I'm old, I suppose. It's not that I can't measure time; it's just that I don't care enough to.

So here I am, dying.

I lie down to make it easier, flat on my side with my neck pressed against the ground. This is how calves and foals sleep—artlessly and abandoned to their rest. I wheeze into the dust. There are footsteps coming towards me and I wonder if my master is going to attempt to whip me back to health, or worse still, shorten my dying. Let my death be my own, at least.

My memories of how it began are all tied up with him, even though he wasn't the cause of any of it. Probably it started long before that, when Toyland was built, or when a spell was cast in the woods, or with something that I don't know about at all. He was strange, enchanted—a wooden toy that had come to some semblance of life. I was a boy, then, leaning on a street corner, and he made my skin prickle when I saw him. His face was smooth and polished, a varnished expression painted in place. His eyes were flat. His voice was not. He talked fast and desperately. He was an uncanny thing, asking for directions home like any other lucky fool with one to go to.

But then, I'd seen my fair share of strangeness and took it to be a curse or a spell or even some spirit caught in clockwork. He was an innocent thing. Or stupid. I think I called him stupid at the time.

'What're you?' I'd said, all rough and ready. I spat.

'Me, I'm a puppet I am, made by a man, my father, and I'm alive, I don't look it but I am—'

Babble, babble. He'd do that if you weren't quick to cut him off.

'Alright, whisht now.' I took to him. He reminded me of somebody I used to know. There was an air to him—a sort of hunger so fierce it grabbed and grappled at you. But not like the other hollowed-out young ones and old ones

I'd grown up around; this one wasn't starving for food. 'Ye seem grand,' I said. 'A grand lad.'

His head tilted to one side. 'Yes, like a boy, you know I want to be a boy, the fairy told me I'd be one tomorrow, a real one—'

'Ye'd like it where I'm going,' I said. 'Only the real lads—the real boys—get to go there.'

'Where's this, where's that you're going?' he said, all eager.

'Toyland!' I said. His face was blank. Well, it always looked blank, but when he didn't talk straight away I guessed he was baffled. 'You never heard of Toyland? It's a grand time.' Rumours had been growing, creeping through the streets, flourishing in the tenements and blooming in the alleys. 'They feed you there. Boys don't do enthing but play all day. No work or school or *nothing*.'

'I have to go to school, the fairy told me, it's what good boys do and I have to be good—'

'Ah, the piseogs'll always lead you astray.' I'm sure I would have spat again at this point. I may have even farted for emphasis. The puppet was silent for a while. Perhaps he was impressed by my physical flourishes.

'And who made this place, how are you going there, when?'

'If you come along you can see for yourself. Bet you'll learn more than in a week of school.'

'And the real boys, they go there?'

'Oh yes, indeed they do! Indeed *we* do, amn't I right?'

That had him. He swallowed it up like a duck eating bread. Real boys, that's all he wanted to hear about, that's all he desired to be. Could've told him real boys wore aprons and had babies and he'd be in labour, cooking dinner before you could finish a sentence. I did call him stupid, I remember now.

A donkey's head is far heavier than a boy's. My nose is low to the ground. It's best to keep eyes down, anyway. I am kept alive, just. The collar around my neck rubs me raw. Donkeys don't need a metal bit but the taste of metal in my mouth is not unfamiliar to me.

They put a jenny in the field with me once. They wanted me to sire more donkeys, create some stock, something to sell. I turned from her snuffly nose and wagging ears. She was a donkey, and I was a boy who had been made one. We were not the same.

But in the end I fucked her anyway.

The puppet and I made an unlikely pair. I was big and dirty and hungry enough that I avoided being a target. The puppet, though, he was a victim just begging to be abused. He attracted tricksters and liars and scoundrels. It was like wasps at a picnic.

He'd had some adventures, some capturings and escapings, and he told me all about them in that too-fast, tripping-up way of his. It took me a while to realise why he spoke like that: he had no lungs, of course. Silly me. I listened to him because there was nothing better to do. I did become interested, in the end, if only because I was trying to figure out if all this had really happened to him or if he was mad, or infested with woodworm.

It was no bother finding a way to Toyland.

'Get on board, boys,' said the sinister coachman, opening the door for us.

Did I waver? If I did, it was only for the length of time it took me to spot the bread and meat and bottles set out on the seats. We got in and the coachman leered and merrily whipped his donkeys onwards to Toyland.

The puppet became less strange the longer I was around him. He told me his father and maker had wanted a son. I wanted to ask him what had stopped the man from taking in one of the ragged barefoot children that roamed the town, or from getting some slut pregnant. Someone had unearthed a lump of talking bogwood while cutting turf, and had taken it to the puppet's maker, and the result was sitting across from me in that dusty, chilly coach.

My thoughts move slowly as a donkey. I have caught myself not thinking for days on end, days and days in which I have just been a donkey. Those times are not bad. I am not happy to remember that I can think otherwise; I am never pleased at my return to consciousness. It's easier to be without it.

Toyland, when we got there, was no grand amusement park. It was more like a slum of shabby houses and filthy pubs. I didn't even know where it was but I assumed the midlands. It had a claggy sort of feel to it. By the look of the other boys I could tell our stories would be similarly grim, backgrounds of hunger and beatings and nights in doorways.

The puppet drew attention, alright. Took hardly any time for a gang to approach us with matches in one hand and cruelty in the other.

'Back off, ya bastards!' I shouted valiantly.

'What, are you his brother or something? Yer ma must've needed some real wood after she had you.' It may have been the funniest thing this particular boy had said, ever.

'I don't have a brother,' I said. 'Or a ma, neither.'

'We just wanna see if he feels pain,' said another. He must have had a scientific mind. I saw a tattered cat skulking in a corner and grabbed it.

'Play with this instead.' I shoved the cat at them.

'Ah, we know cats feel pain,' the scientist said.

I'd already dragged the puppet away. We ducked into a pub.

'The cat!' The puppet was twisting his twiggy limbs under my hand, giving me splinters. 'Why did you, why did you give it to them?'

'Shut up,' I said to him, and pulled the door closed behind me so that we wouldn't hear the shrieks of the cat as it was set on fire.

I've been bought and sold several times. It's a nerve-wracking time, being brought to the mart. The sellers trot us out and prospective buyers wedge our jaws open to look at our teeth. Between my own inspections, I would look at the other donkeys and wonder which ones I would buy, if I were a boy again. I've decided now that I wouldn't buy a donkey at all; I would much prefer a horse.

I always tried to look good for the men who seemed a bit gentler. Pushed my nose to their hands and hoped I'd get a good master. Snapped at the men I didn't like. I've daydreamed about being bought by a girl, one who would take me home to a stable and brush me down and rub my ears with her soft little hands. But a girl like that would never visit the grubby small town markets that things like me are sold at.

And in the end one master is much the same as any other.

Toyland was a fine old time. We were carefree boys, with no rules or responsibilities, coming into the prime of our teenage years. It was, as a result, a violent and volatile place. There were brawls, and gangs that were quick to form and even quicker to dissolve.

The majority of our time we spent in the run-down pubs. There were never any barmen, just a seemingly endless supply of watery stout. There was tobacco too, and cheap cigars. I partook in all of it, though the puppet didn't. He generally just kept me company while I drank myself to the lively point of vomit and unconsciousness. When I awoke he would still be there and we would carry on.

We rarely saw any grown-ups, though they must have been around to restock and supply our vices. One day we came upon a gang of boys who had found some opium and I passed some hours in a haze of vertigo and nightmares. None of us missed an adult presence; we were doing just grand on our own.

The puppet might have missed his father. He talked about him often enough. He never said he wanted to leave, though. He just kept asking me if he was a real boy yet.

'Yer certainly getting closer,' I would slur. 'This is wha' real boys *do*.'

'But I don't look any different, do I, or feel any different, I feel the same—'

'Give it time,' I said. 'You won't feel different straight away. Give it a bit more time.'

Once after saying this, or something like it, I remember getting sick into my glass and throwing it at some other boy's head. We had a fight and then I kept on drinking.

We were there for about a fortnight before I became a donkey. I remember that very well. I was sitting at a table, scoffing soda bread and sausages with my hands, laughing at something or someone, ha-ha-ha-ing with my mouth full and open. It must have been a good joke, because I was still laughing when the change began. It was not my ears that grew first, but my hooves.

My toes went numb and then it felt as though there was a crust over my feet, hardening and setting like melted wax when you dip a finger into it and let it cool in the air. Then the strangeness was in my hands, and I saw what must have happened to my feet; my fingers stuck together and my nails grew right over them and over the backs of my hands, swelling, darkening, setting themselves into little black hooves.

I screamed and screamed. My backbone stretched and my knees twisted unnaturally until they were the wrong side of my legs. Then my ears grew. They pushed themselves up my skull to the top of my head. Hair burst from everywhere. I shrieked and howled and had broken the table already, smashing food to the floor, sobbing at the faces around me that looked on, blurrily astonished and idiotic.

By then, of course, it was far too late. But I was still screaming.

'Help, help me! Please, please, please. Help, help, heeeee—heeeeee—' and as I drew my breath in my vocal cords must have changed too, for I brayed a dreadful, 'Heeee haaaaaw!'

And then I could speak no more. I cried and cried, frightened by my own unrecognisable noise and by the realisation that donkeys don't cry tears.

The puppet was flailing his limbs around and shouting his babble, but he was mostly ignored. The same transformation had begun to take hold of some of the other boys in the room, and the rest ran away. A few, high on a cloud of opium, sat in a corner and watched it all, no doubt thinking that this was all just part of the dream.

I shivered out my shock in a little wooden pen that was full of other newly made donkeys. We had been swiftly rounded up with whips and cattle prods. They must have been ready and waiting.

I stared at the planks I was pressed against and saw that there were teeth marks in the wood, and clumps of grey donkey hair, and blood. Some men came in and shouted and jabbed sharp sticks into the sides of the more hysterical donkeys.

'Ouch, would ya stop!'

I shivered when I realised that one of the donkeys could still speak.

'Ah here! We've got a chatty one!' said one of the men. They opened the gate and grabbed him.

'Please!' the donkey said, all wild and white-eyed. 'Please—let me go home!'

'Home?' One of the men holding the donkey laughed. 'Like this? You'd give your ma a shock!'

'My ma!' The donkey shook beneath the men's rough hands and cried, 'Mammy, mammy!'

The men dragged the talking donkey away. I don't know what they did with him.

I don't know what happened to the puppet either. He hadn't turned into a donkey; he already had a spell on him. Wood could only take so much. Most likely he got away. He was so stupid he was probably fine. Stupid people can get on remarkably well in life.

And now as I feel my breath fall out I think the curse is loosening its hold on me. My hooves are pinning and needling me and they are softening, splitting apart to form fingers and toes again. My dusty grey hair falls away. I am shrinking. I am becoming a little thin figure like the other people I see. I fear I may blow away.

There is a figure over me. Not my master. Some boy. He puts a hand on my arm. His skin looks very pale against mine. He's got a round, stupid face. The puppet, I think. And then, no, it couldn't be. This boy is too young. He's not the puppet. Just a boy. Firm flesh and unbroken bones. He stands and looks down at me. Wipes his hand on his trousers. Walks away.

Is he leaving me? I try to raise my head a little. That's too hard to do, so I rest it back on the ground again. But my voice must have returned to me, like the rest of my human parts. I want him to come back. Give me help, or pity, or mercy. My mouth hangs loose, my tongue moves, trying to cry out but nothing happens. I want to say that I've been good, but I've forgotten how to speak, that I'm a boy, really, but I don't know how to say it.

Dollhouse

One doll turned in place to the imagined song
of a music box. One sat at a miniature table
mouthing daintily at her ceramic meal. The last
stood motionless by the dollhouse door, jointed limbs
stiffly poised. Each a perfect porcelain Goldilocks.

The dollmaker's voice was bear growl
through the empty window frames. The dollmother
picked apart elbows, pried painted glass eyes
from their sockets, stuffed bellies with cotton.
She posed the dolls on metal stands.

At night she swallowed her own eyes, stopped
up her ears with tallow and hid from their seeking.

The three dolls drew their floral curtains
tight and sucked at bonbons. The dollhouse filled
with the stretch of hollow mouths, the weighted blink
of horsehair eyelashes. Each morning the dollmaker
stripped them to see if they were bleeding yet.

Rachel Plummer

The Great Hunger
Roisín O'Donnell

We are the watching eyes of the Irish wilderness. Its panting tongue. Its quickening pulse. Its teeth. The ancient Irish called us *mac tír*—sons of the land. And it was Ireland that forged us, from our granite pelts and frost-white muzzles, to our turf-dark noses and shifting, sky-coloured eyes. We belong here, no less than the hawks of the high peaks or the ravenous pike of the still waters. Our night-song sent thrills through children's dreams. Our glimpsed silhouettes were revered. And in huddles at the moonlit crossroads, people would whisper our legends. Deer were plentiful then, and the forests were creaking with life. We never hungered for human flesh, with its caked-in carcinogens and sweet fattiness. We never wished the Irish ill, until they started to invent stories with which to kill us off.

They said we were sharp-fanged and vicious. That we preyed on children, disguising ourselves as their grandmothers. They said we were mercenaries for hire—the *Laignach Faelad*—and that we'd only accept payment in the form of the flesh of newborns.

One murder starts a genocide. Within a century, we'd been wiped out, and even the rivers changed course.

Now the time has come for our return.

Humans call it the 'sixth sense', but there are so many levels of perception they know nothing about. We sense a woman coming from the New World, driven by a hunger almost as great as ours. We see the deltas of blue veins on her pale wrists. She is sitting on a metal bird in the sky, squinting against hard sunlight above clouds. She swallows to quench the ache in her chest. Her hands grip each other and she watches the map in front of her, a red ember pulsing across an ocean signposted with shipwrecks. She doesn't realise each maritime disaster draws her closer to us.

*

'Skaiste!' Her name means 'sky' in a language her ancestors once spoke.

Her Irish mate holds her, drinking her in. 'Welcome home,' he says. 'Good flight?'

She forces a smile. 'Great.'

In their stony den, the two fall into each other. Humans don't only couple during one season, as we do. We mate when the rivers are high, when stags lock antlers and red grouse fly startled from the bilberry bushes. But humans are driven by craving for each other's bodies all year round. No wonder they make such stupid choices.

Like us, humans are supposed to mate for life, but long ago, this woman had another mate, in her other life across the ocean. Skaiste has never told her Irish partner about the child she carried for months and how it died inside her. How her abdomen became a tomb of bones for the rotting fruit of her womb. How, when she sat on the ice-block bathroom floor of her Phoenix apartment with the blood seeping out of her, before she dialled an ambulance, before she even screamed, she thought about how some animals eat their deceased young, and wondered what this would taste like. She has never told him how snowflakes grazed the frosted window. In Arizona. For the first time in her life. *Snow*.

She shivers. In the stony den, sweat cools on the backs of her naked thighs.

'Skaiste?' Her mate turns her to face him. 'So, when are we going to start trying?'

She tries not to react, tries not to roll him over and pin him down and take from him the thing she's wanted ever since she sat on that ice-cold floor with its tiles no longer white but red.

There is a hunger that scalds.

Humans have all seen it and pretended not to. That smug back-in-shape mummy jogging a something-month-old on her hip as she waits to pay at the till. The sales assistant who doesn't say *how old* or *how cute*, but just folds the woman's receipt, and without blinking, passes over her change. For every woman cooing over a stranger's baby, there's another at a safe distance wondering what that infant's skull would look like split.

Unlike us, humans love to deny their instincts, salivating only for things removed from reach. Skaiste never wanted a child until she lost one. She spent her most fertile years taking pills to keep her infertile, but still a child took seed. Now the yearning for offspring is a tapeworm eroding her internally.

She is the one who will bear witness. Her hunger is savage enough to have brought her here, and it will bring her to us.

*

The night of our release is pitch and stabbed with stars.

The Irish mate wears a T-shirt embossed with the silhouette of a wolf and the emblem GROWWL—*Group for the Reintroduction of Wolves into the Wicklow Locality*. He and Skaiste join hands with the others, forming a human wall of rustling legs and squeaking boots that herd us into a corner of our enclosure. We are blanketed, pricked with needles, bundled into massive crates and put into the backs of Land Rovers. When they drive in convoy into the dark mountains, Skaiste's chest tightens.

'Don't worry, honey.' Her mate rubs her thigh. 'It's been carefully planned.'

Honey? As if there were any sweetness left in her.

We can feel the nearness of our homeland. We slabber and ache with the hunger of years.

On the hilltop, humans stand around with searchlights. When they open the doors, the land rises up to meet us, bitter and fresh and pungent with coming rain. As soon as our crates are opened, we bolt with our ears back, as if running from ourselves.

It's somewhat of an anti-climax. Humans stub their toes, and Skaiste pulls her partner's arm. 'Is that it?'

The night is still. The only trace of us is the scent on crate bars, and tufts of fur floating ominously from the skeletal tendrils of ferns. 'Bloody Lake?' someone suggests, and the humans rally again. Suck-slam the jeep doors echo, and they drive back down the hill, congratulating themselves on their magnanimous gesture.

Unleashed, we have found a trampled island.

In our absence, the Sika deer have grown fearless, their interloper eyes scanning rocky outcrops. Only the odd tractor sends them skipping up the mountain with the white heart- shapes of their arses flashing. Sheep wander stupidly between heather, filling the hills with droning bleats. Plant life has been chewed and farmed into a bland pitch without the flavours of thyme, fennel and wild garlic that used to dance into our nostrils, making us sing.

Everything is flattened now. Trees have been cleared and the wind is merciless.

'It's positive!' Skaiste smiles through briny tears. The two mates stare at each other; cats in a dark alley.

'So soon,' he says. 'I didn't think… You hear of couples trying for…'

She laughs. 'Luck, I suppose.'

He doesn't know she's been charting her inner workings, just as the ancient

Irish built burial chambers by calculating the sunrise. He cannot let the thought dawn; that none of their couplings have ever been spontaneous. That those nights when she came to him with the fullness of her pale pelt uncovered were carefully planned, orchestrated in accordance with the moon. Who would allow themselves ponder the notion that hunger can chase away love?

Soon, her body starts changing. The areolas around her nipples darken. Fang-sharp pains bite into her temples. Crimson claw-lines scar her hips. She starts to dream. Other pregnant women dream of eating earth, but Skaiste dreams of teeth. She sees herself climbing into a swirling blizzard that parts to reveal a wolf tearing into a fresh kill. Blood oozes between its paws, and she doesn't know what type of animal it has caught. She's drawn towards the hot meaty smell of the prey, trying to ascertain what kind of animal it could be. But every time the kill comes into focus, she wakes, sweating and too terrified to weep. Naked, she clutches her belly like a fortune teller's globe and stares at the frost-white ceiling.

'Honey. Are you *okay*?' her mate asks one morning as they sit in the sunlit kitchen, stirring breakfast porridge neither of them are eating. 'You've been so…'

'It's nothing,' she says automatically, looking up from a book of wolf legends. Then the need in his eyes makes her buckle. 'This is gonna sound nuts, but it's just the wolves… the ones we released into Wicklow? I can't stop thinking about them. You sure it was okay, releasing them like that?'

'Of course,' he says, relieved it's nothing worse.

He tells her how wolf-reintroduction has been done in Yellowstone. They've reported natural control of deer numbers, greater biodiversity and a boost in tourism figures. 'If you like, we can go for a walk one day? Check up on our wolfies? If we're lucky enough to see them, that is. They're very shy. People have been having a hard time spotting them. We're not quite sure where they've gone.' He nuzzles her neck. 'Don't worry, honey. We'll go find them, make you feel better.'

'I'd like that,' she says. They both grimace, fake smiles to nullify each other's unspoken fears, but then life intervenes.

Their son is born early with blood on his lungs. Famished for so long, for a living child instead of a pooling red mess, Skaiste feels time stop. For the next three weeks she doesn't know if it's day or night, or what strange creatures stalk the corridors of her mind.

There's a fear that's never fully recovered from. From our frothing saliva, rivers were formed. Shape-shifter warriors. Mercenaries paid in the tender meat of newborns. In Skaiste's New World, the Skin Walkers of the Navajo channel courage through their hooded pelts. While she was heavy with child, she read of Lycaon, turned into a wolf as punishment for eating his offspring. From Greek mythology to Nordic legends, humans do not fear the wolf so much as the wolf part in all of them.

A part that, once turned, might not turn back.

Four months later, she sits on the seafront at Bray, rocking her son's pram and watching him breathing. Everything feels far away, as if she's looking out from behind a waterfall. She squints at the horizon, tries to bring it into focus, returns her stare to the infant. At first, this child was too sick to name. Even now that they have plucked a word to call him, Skaiste hesitates to use it; as if afraid it might hurt him somehow.

'Honey?' her mate touches her hand, rigor-mortised around the pram handle. 'You have to relax. The nurse said he's grand, right?'

She nods.

'Come on. You should be enjoying the fresh air, the...'

She stills his arm. 'What kind of dog is that?'

'Umm...' he says. 'Is it some kind of German Shepherd?'

Under the candy-striped umbrellas of the Cereal Killer Café, a grey animal lolls across the pavement. Beside it, a young woman with a tasselled handbag sips foamy coffee from a tall glass and absent-mindedly pats the animal's head. Yellow eyes swoop. The animal stops panting and stares. For Skaiste, it is the creature's proportions that chill her. Its ears are the height of her son's plastic bottles with their yellow teats, its tail the length of his wicker Moses basket. The animal licks its jowls, and the young woman feeds it another quarter of her poppy-seed muffin.

Skaiste grips the handle tighter. 'That is not a German Shepherd. That is a fucking wolf.'

'Okay, okay. Listen,' he says, hands up in surrender. 'I didn't want to worry you. But there's been a slight... well. *Situation* with the wolves.'

January. The wolf moon. The Inuit call it that because all other animals are sleeping. Only our baying can be heard over the winter stillness. And that's when we began coming into the towns. At first people were afraid. A couple of us were tranquilised and re-released deeper into the hills. But we'd always return and sit outside people's doors, whining cutely. One clever wolf even rescued a child who'd dashed in front of a lorry in the Lidl carpark, and that was the start of it.

'I guess they're not as wild as we thought,' he laughs. 'They're really quite tame. Lots of people have taken them in as pets. They're very obedient. Great with kids.'

Skaiste stares at him. 'Have you lost your mind? We need to have them all put down. This is fucking dangerous.'

'Honey, relax. There's been no one hurt. They're very friendly. I promise.'

But with the telepathic certainty in her belly that told her she was bearing a child, she can see through our plan to endear ourselves to the local population. Now, nearly every house in Wicklow has a 'pet wolfie' who drools under the kitchen table, leaps for frisbees in the park and lazes by the television. We parade the promenade at Greystones, bejewelled with stylish rhinestone collars to match our owners' handbags, or pace alongside joggers on their morning power-runs. We are fast becoming status symbols. And each night, we hurdle over garden walls, gnaw through hedges and tear through heather to meet by the shores of heart-shaped Lough Ouler at the top of Tonlegee Mountain. At the point where, if it were a real heart, it would break.

She knows. But—*It's okay, Skaiste, don't worry, Skaiste. A little boy, Skaiste! You must be so happy, Skaiste*—why does no one listen? Are they fucking crazy? Nauseated by *Caring For Your Newborn* instructing her how to be a good mother, by people telling her how to feel, she will prove the threat we pose is not just in her mind. What about that missing Arklow two-year-old from the news? Or the Roundwood farmer whose lambs vanished overnight? There must be carcasses in those hills. The ivory lantern of a small sheep's nibbled skull. A toddler's pelvis, licked clean. One bright May evening, she grabs her camera, ties her child to her front like a clinging bear cub, and sets out into the mountains.

Spring is in full frenzy. Tourists pull into lay-bys to take photographs of mountains that refuse to be captured, each vista outdone by the next. But to Skaiste, the Irish landscape is ravenous. Hedgerows slobber with frothy white blossoms. Pus-yellow gorse erupts over fields. Pines gasp into shapes of yawning jowls. Everything attacks her senses. Crows call, mocking children's cries. Her son whimpers in response.

She pats his back and keeps on climbing.

At first she doesn't notice the absence of spring, or the soft coldness against her cheek as winter descends onto Tonlegee Mountain.

The whiteness is sudden. In the haze, patterns of ice and rocks take on the shapes of teeth, tongues and watching eyes.

'Fuck.' Skaiste turns back, blinded by the thickening fog. Which way is home? Heart loud in her head, she tries to focus on securing each step, on ground covered with a slick afterbirth of frost. Sleet stings her cheeks, causing a scattering of sound, of feelings.

Skaiste we're sorry   miscarriage   sometimes it just
body rejects
no real reason   tea, you want
Skaiste not your fault   you just have to   tea
it's just   body rejects

She's almost at Lough Ouler when the snap of a twig makes her turn.

We step out of the mist.

Before she remembers fear, her first reaction is awe. How beautiful we are. How soft. Our eyes take the evening light and disembowel it into its components. Now red, now indigo, now white. Our howling song speaks to something inside her; a pain she's been carrying for so long.

Nowhere to hide on the mountain, barren but for a single twisted sapling. In the pause between heartbeats, we have her surrounded.

Her camera slides in her sweaty grip. With each blink of her eyes, our image changes. Now canine, snarling on all fours. Now upright; towering men with matted hair, ragged capes and hardened jaws, pointing blood-rusted spears at her throat. But we are weak, our skins pale, our muscles wizened. Some of us boast ugly welts of unhealed battle scars.

Mirrored in Skaiste's eyes, every wolf legend she's read becomes manifest. We are the *Laignach Faelad*, begotten in the imaginations of the ancient Irish. No longer *mac tír*, sons of the land, but wolf-shifter warriors, mercenaries for hire. With their story, the Irish justified their brutality, whispering our legend so often it became true. Our spirits attached themselves to the lithe grey bodies of the Irish wolves. In naming us, the Irish breathed life into us.

As wolf and as man, the hunger Skaiste sees in our faces is the same. It will only be sated when we have received our payment. And the fee we require is blood compensation for two-hundred-and-thirty years. Two-hundred-and-thirty years since the last of us was shot, leaving our disembodied spirits drifting across Ireland, looking for wolf forms onto which we could attach ourselves. Two-hundred-and-thirty years until two crates of Alaskan Timber wolves were released into the Wicklow hills. Two-hundred-and-thirty years of hunting denied us. Two-hundred-and-thirty years burning in purgatory, while we waited to return. No gold. No silver. No credit cards. We will only accept payment in one form.

She drops her camera, clutches the child to her.

'Listen,' she says. As if we could be reasoned with.

She, of all humans, must realise hunger is a cunning creature, not easily appeased. Years of baptisms and children's birthday parties. Years spent pretending to smile into prams. Even now, as she clasps the head of the son she is supposed to love, Skaiste feels her chest ache for the one she lost. Forcing one life into existence cannot make up for the loss of another. The few lives of a single pack cannot atone for the annihilation of our ancestors. At the very least, we require retribution.

No one will see us come. Down culs-de-sac and mews. Into homes where we have made ourselves welcome. *Honey, our wolfie's at the door! Better let him in.* One first payment is all we need to begin regaining our strength.

We watch Skaiste's thoughts dart across her eyes. She understands. We are the *Laignach Faelad*. If she gives us the child, we will release her. She could untie the sling, drop the heavy burden of this placebo who's failed to sate her hunger. She could run back down the mountain, to warm relief, buttered toast, a long hot bath. Her mate will not be home for hours. She could forget—

No.

Horrified, she stumbles backwards. We part, letting her pass, and follow; our paws pad silently through snow.

What creatures dwell in her mind to make her think such things?

What kind of person would conceive such a thought?

She grips her child tight, too tight.

We paw closer, our growls magnificent. Our breath steams onto her skin.

Her child struggles for air.

Cornered, she backs into the gnarled clutch of the twisted sapling. Spindly branches claw her hair. A lone raven wheels above, cackling. Wind roars. Our drool glistens. Skaiste's hands let go of her child's fading warmth. Her fingers start to shake.

Rowan berries burst, blood clots against snow.

Icy flurries catch our fur. Life surges through our veins. Our howls echo into the eternal silence of our island. We have returned.

Troll Song

'I went walking out today, Mama,
Took the road right down to the wood.
A troll man spoke from under the bridge
Saying he'd fix me up good.'

                                        'He just wants attention, darling,
                                          He doesn't really mean it, dear.
                                            You'll feel an awful lot better
                                        If you pretend like you can't hear.'

'I went walking out today, Papa,
Took the path out to the loch.
A troll man came up from the reeds,
Asked if I'd suck on his cock.'

                                 'The world is a dangerous place, poppet,
                                          Not made for my pretty child,
                                 But you'll be safe if you stay indoors
                                     And don't venture out in the wild.'

'I went walking out today, brother,
Took the trail up round the cape.
A troll man stood on the shore,
Preaching the virtues of rape.'

                                              'It was clearly in jest, sissy,
                                           Where's your sense of humour?
                                        Maybe you should see a quack;
                                   You're wired like you've got a tumour.'

'I went walking out today, cousin,
Took the track that runs by the ditch.
A troll man walked after me,
Called me a whore and a bitch.'

                                            'You musta provoked him, silly,
                                          Looking the way that you do.
                               Nice girls don't get comments like that,
                                    So what he said musta been true.'

'I went out the house today, sister,
Stood by our front door,
Knifed up the troll man waiting for me
And now I'm going to war.'

                                                'Arm yourself, my sister,
                                               And I shall do the same,
                               You get the matches, I'll get the pitch,
                                 And we'll put this house to flame.'

Natasha Calder

The Fire at the Ritz
Brendan Murphy

A charming lady

Sometimes life is stranger than fiction. In 1992, I was a freelance journalist—mostly writing local interest stories for the *Liverpool Echo*. That September I did a two-page spread on 'The Silver Screens of Yesteryear'—a nostalgia piece fondly documenting some of the old picture palaces in the Merseyside area. It was after reading my article that a Mrs Sally Murgatroyd contacted me. On the phone she informed me that she was, in fact, the daughter of Henry Sutton, the last manager of the Ritz cinema in Birkenhead (one of the cinemas I'd written about). She said that if I cared to meet her the following week, she had a story I might be interested in.

I found Sally to be a charming engaging lady, then in her late sixties, although age had done nothing to dim her sparkle. She spoke lovingly of her father and the cinema he had managed. In its day the Ritz was regarded as one of the best theatres outside London's West End. Of course, this was the era of cine-variety, when the presentation of live acts between films had been a regular part of the cinema-going experience. The Ritz had been purpose-built for cine-variety and soon gained a reputation as the 'Showplace of the North', well known for attracting the top variety acts of the day and the biggest names in radio. From my own research, I already knew that the Ritz had been a prestigious venue—a monument, almost, to civic pride.[1] Unfortunately (as I reported in my piece) the building had burnt down on Valentine's Day, 1932.

After we'd talked for about an hour, Sally finally turned the conversation around to the fire. I'd been led to believe that the blaze had started in the projection room (nitrate film is notoriously flammable) but Sally informed

---

[1] Constructed on an island site of over an acre, the building's frontage had been faced with white Portland stone, while on the corner over the main entrance, a circular steel-and-glass tower rose seventy feet into the air (see Fig. 1, p. 74). At night this would be magnificently illuminated in red and green.

me this was not the case. The tale she went on to tell, quite frankly, I found incredulous—an absurd yarn, involving the blanket conspiracy of a whole town. Wistfully she said it was a shame I could not have spoken with her husband, Johnny, who could have corroborated her story, but he had died some years previously.

Sally herself passed away not long after I had interviewed her. For some reason, maybe out of respect, I kept the tape of our conversation.

'Silliness'

I thought nothing more of that chat for over twenty years. Then, two years ago, I read in the *Wirral Globe* that the Birkenhead Police Department had found the private journal of one Pat Grimshaw, formerly Desk Sergeant and a well-respected officer who would go on to become Inspector before he retired in 1955.[2] The *Globe* article drew attention to the 'silliness' of Grimshaw's entry for 14th February 1932. As I read the date, something in my memory stirred. The next day, I went down to the Police Station and asked if I could take a look at Grimshaw's journal for myself. What I found confirmed everything that Sally Murgatroyd (née Sutton) had told me.

After two years of verifying all the facts, I now feel it is nothing less than my humane duty to reveal exactly how—and why—the Ritz cinema burnt to the ground all those years ago. But I must warn you: as a serious journalist, my primary objective is to reveal the truth—no matter what pain and anxiety that may cause. So with that in mind, I will make public for the first time, the undisguised facts of what occurred that night. These facts may shock you. They may offend you. But know this—you are reading the truth.

Exuberant mood

To fully understand the origins of the events of 14th February 1932, we must first take an imaginative leap in time and space and go back to the kitchen of a modest terrace house on Hoylake Road, Birkenhead, where Henry Sutton, manager of the Ritz, sat at the kitchen table with his eight-year-old daughter, Sally. As Sally was to recall during our interview, her father was in exuberant mood that day, eagerly waiting for his son, Billy, to come out from the front

---

[2] The discovery of Inspector Grimshaw's journal had occurred while the police had been searching through their old paper files, then being digitally transcribed for the public to access on the internet.

room where he was trying on a new costume. It was a bleak Sunday afternoon and Sally later remembered with sadness that it would be the last time she would be in the company of either of them.

"Ey! Our Billy! You ready yet?' Henry shouted.

'Yeah,' the lad called out.

'Come on then. Let's be having you.'

As Billy Sutton lumbered into the kitchen, Sally let out a yelp. Henry Sutton, in contrast, was beaming. As for Billy, he just stood there—eighteen years of age, six foot two and dreadful! Truly, horrifically, dreadful! The sharp bony ridges of his face were shaded bluish green, the colour of a long-dead corpse; the top of his skull looked as if it had been sawn straight across, then closed flat like a box. And (what Sally remembered the most) this suffering seemed to be mirrored in his red watery eyes—the suffering of a crazed creature half-dead, half-alive.

'Dad, do I have to wear this? I look bloody stupid.'

'Nonsense lad, you look grand.'

By all accounts, it was an ingenious costume design. The idea had been to dress Billy up as Frankenstein's monster. They had fashioned the now legendary flat-topped head by asking a friend who worked at Cammel Laird's Shipbuilders to weld two tin side plates on to a small biscuit tin, which would then sit comfortably on Billy's head like a square helmet. A couple of towels were laid across his neck and shoulders, with a big, ancient blazer worn over them to give him that lurching thick-set look. The arms of the blazer and the hems on his trousers were cut short to make his limbs appear unnaturally large. Finally, to add height, he wore massive diver's boots (once again, generously provided by Henry's friend at Cammel Laird's). [3]

---

[3] Perhaps a note of explanation is needed here: The main feature to be screened that night was none other than the Hollywood classic *Frankenstein* (it had premiered in New York in December 1931 and, as was normal in those days, had taken two months to cross the Atlantic). To celebrate the occasion, Henry thought it would be a hoot to have Billy come on stage after the film had finished, dressed as the monster. It would be the icing on the cake after an already extravagant evening of entertainment—a bit of a laugh at the end of the night.

One must remember that the Ritz had been fully equipped for the most elaborate stage presentations. Its stage was 75 foot wide and the cine-screen had been fitted with rollers at the base, allowing it to be moved back and forth along grooved tracks in the floor. Henry Sutton had spared no efforts in justifying the title 'Showplace of the North' for his theatre. Although he had dedicated his life to the cinema industry, Henry's true passion was for the stage—it was often said that he was 'a born showman'—and it was probably this innate sense of showmanship that had led him to dress his son up as Boris Karloff.

'Dad! I feel like a right prat! William Henry Prat! That's what they're going to call me.'

'Don't be daft, lad, no one will recognise you. I hardly recognise you meself.'

'Oh God.'

'Now remember, I want you at the picture house at half ten at the latest. I want you on that stage, full costume at eleven o'clock. I'll give you a nod and you can follow me on.'

And so…

Generator of dreams

On that fateful Sunday evening, the Ritz cinema loomed high above the rain-soaked slate roofs of Birkenhead like a giant power plant—a generator of dreams—a retailer of hope—as the 7 o'clock queue snaked halfway down Conway Street. How could anyone have known that the countdown to disaster had already started? Through my interview with Sally and my other extensive research, I have managed to piece together a rough timeline of the tragic events that night. To the best of my knowledge this is what happened:

- 7.15pm: Two Popeye cartoons.
- 7.40pm: The Dagenham Girl Pipers and Drummers.
- 8.00pm: Newsreel.
- 8.30pm: Jan Ralfini and his Broadcasting Band.
- 9.00pm: Steffani and his 21 Singing Songsters.
- 9.30pm: Interval (in which Mr Reginald Forte introduced and demonstrated the Compton Grand Organ).
- 10.00pm: The main feature film—*Frankenstein*.

At 10.35pm, Billy Sutton arrived at the Ritz, having spent the last hour in the Argyle pub. Meanwhile, in the main auditorium a full capacity of 2500 people sat frozen, watching the film. How easily the collective psyche is mesmerised by shadows of dark and light that dance on a rectangular screen. How easily the human mind falls into that two-dimensional world! How easily we submit our senses to celluloid—its time, its place, its make-believe window of reality. Who can say what hypnotic effect this remarkable film had on its audience that night?[4]

Watching the film that night was sixteen-year-old Kitty Reilly, on her first date with local boy Johnny Murgatroyd. We can picture Johnny as he sat there, entranced; his thick-rimmed, penny-round glasses reflecting the strobe-like flashing white images; his mouth slightly agape as, on screen, the monster's birth gathers momentum…

The table is finally lowered. One hand, limp, lifeless, hangs over the table's edge. For what seems like an eternity, nothing happens. Then the fingers begin to twitch.

'It's alive—it's alive—IT'S ALIVE!' cries Frankenstein.

Perfectly attired

11pm: At the end of the film, the credits rolled. The screen ran blank, the houselights went up and the peach satin curtains glided across the stage.

---

[4] And it is a remarkable film. Universal Studio's *Frankenstein*, directed by James Whale, is not only a masterpiece of the horror genre, it's an all-time classic. The 'birth' scene is still ranked as one of the finest in cinematic history—often imitated, but never bettered. It is probably the most iconic ten minutes of any horror film. A short refresher for readers who may not be familiar with it:

As a storm rages over the abandoned windmill in which Frankenstein is conducting his experiments, he is suddenly interrupted by his fiancée, Elizabeth, his friend, Victor Moritz, and his one-time tutor and mentor, Dr Waldman. The famous sequence begins when Dr Waldman questions the validity of his former pupil's endeavours. (Dr Waldman is played by Edward Van Sloan and Colin Clive is Frankenstein).

In stark monochrome, Dr Waldman looks directly at the camera and asks with grim countenance: 'And you really believe you can bring life to the dead?'

'That body is not dead,' asserts Frankenstein. 'It has never lived. I made it. I created it—from bodies I took from graves, the gallows, anywhere! Go—see for yourself!' He swirls the sheet from the body on the table and stares at the horrified faces of his witnesses. 'Quite a good scene, isn't it? One man crazy, three very sane spectators.'

KERRACK-ARRACK-RACKKK!

On cue, to explosive claps of thunder and lightning, Frankenstein turns to his hunch-backed assistant, Fritz. They rush to operate the mad, monolithic mechanisms that surround them. Dials are turned; levers thrown downwards; jumping electrical currents zig-zag from generator to generator as blinding arcs of chaotic voltage fizzle up, down, and around the machinery, waltzing to a crackling cacophony of white noise.

KERRRACK-ARRACK-RACKKK!

Amidst the mayhem and noise, the trestle, with its hideous burden, is slowly cranked upwards, rising above the heads of those below—rising up to the open skylight—

Where it stops—silhouetted against the crescendo of white lightning that fills the space around it.

Kitty Reilly started putting on her coat:

'It wasn't that scary, was it, Johnny? The film? It wasn't that scary?'

'Eh... No.' Johnny, still seated, shut his mouth and straightened his glasses. 'No, not at all.'

At that point, Henry Sutton, perfectly attired, as usual, in his best suit, stepped out on stage to give his announcements:

'LADIES AND GENTLEMEN—PLEASE— IF I MAY... Please, ladies and gentlemen, thank you. If I could just have your attention for a moment...'

All eyes were on stage.

'I'd just like to remind you that next weekend we have a special screening...'

A loud, clumping sound, like heavy footsteps. Some heard it. Some thought they heard it. Everyone ignored it.

'... a great picture from MGM called *A Free Soul*. It's a courtroom drama starring Norma Shearer...'

An inarticulate moan! Stuttering footsteps echoing around the theatre. Everyone heard that!

'... Lionel Barrymore and Clark Gable...'

Clump! Clump! CLUMP! CLUMP! CLUMP!

A hand appeared from behind the curtain. The thing that followed it...

The thing that followed it was beyond the comprehension of everyone.

And yet, there it was.

What was once a figment of film fantasy had now somehow manifested itself into the material world!

The monster!

Jesus Christ! It's the monster!

RUN! RUN! RUN FOR YOUR LIVES!

Who knows what primal terror erupted in the audience that night as Billy stood there in his biscuit-tin head? Back in 1932, the fear must have been like something those people had never known. Instantly, blind panic spread like wildfire. Many were wounded in the crazed clamour for the exit. One can only imagine Billy, bemused, stuck still on stage in his big boots, while Henry Sutton unsuccessfully tried to appeal for calm. It must have taken no more than ninety seconds for the whole building to be evacuated. In shocked silence, father and son looked out over the devastation. Seats had been ripped out; the beautiful stucco relief on the walls torn down; light fittings left hanging by a wire; the auditorium double doors practically off their hinges.

'They've gone mad,' said Henry Sutton.

'Bloody hell,' said Billy.

Just then, they heard the weak voice of a girl: '... help me... please somebody, help me.'

Without stopping to think and still wearing his Frankenstein helmet, Billy unburdened himself of his boots and ran down the side of the stage to the aisles.

Having lost Johnny, Kitty Reilly had been knocked unconscious by the demented tidal wave of people fighting to get out. She was just coming round, half-concussed, when Billy arrived at the end of the row of seats.

'Here,' he said. 'Come here. I won't hurt you.'

Kitty took one look at him and screamed.

No one entirely knows whether Kitty Reilly had been naturally inclined to a weak heart. But it's more than likely that it was at that moment that the poor girl suffered the cardiac arrest that would kill her.

The monster had claimed its first victim.

Outlandish

Driven by who knows what and probably in a sense of panic, Billy gathered up the girl's body in his arms and carried her out into the foyer. When he saw what was on the streets outside, he laid the girl down and ran back to the auditorium in shock.

'Dad! Dad! There's hundreds of people out there!'

What now follows is taken from the private journal of Police Sgt Grimshaw, Desk Sergeant on duty at Birkenhead Police Station that night:

I'd been called to a disturbance at the Ritz Picture House in Birkenhead at around 11.20pm. An unruly rabble had already gathered around the premises, and more townspeople were joining the throng by the minute. They carried flaming torches, bread knives, spanners, wrenches, garden spades, rakes — anything that could be used in defence against the creature. Initially, I thought the reports of 'a monster' a bit outlandish, to say the least. Then I saw the thing with my own eyes. Pushing my way to the front doors of the cinema, I arrived just in time to witness the fiend striding into the foyer — the battered corpse of an infant in his arms! He dropped the body to the ground, like a warning never to enter, before skulking back into the shadows. I was the senior officer on duty that night and there was no time to call for reinforcements! A decision had to be made at ground level, on the spot. 'We're going in!' I declared to the assembled

crowd. 'We're going in to confront the monster!'
'Kill the monster! Kill the monster!' They chanted in unison.[5]

Billy and his father were inside, no doubt deciding what to do next, when what was left of the double doors smashed open, and a riot of faces burst in.

'There he is!' cried one of the marauding avengers, a robust man in a white vest. 'There's the dark alchemist and his twisted creature spawned from the rotting flesh of innocent victims. Behold! Frankenstein and his creation!'

'Now, hold on a minute, you've got this all wrong—' said Henry Sutton

Tragically, his protestations fell on deaf ears. Later, it would be said that ten to twelve burly men descended upon him.

Inferno

Meanwhile, Billy was making a run for it; out of the main arena, and up toward the fire escape. A few men started after him, but were quickly stopped by the leader: 'No! Listen to me! The only way to stop a demon born in hell is to send it back there! Burn down this evil place! Burn down this laboratory of madness! The monster will trouble us no more!'

'BURN IT DOWN! BURN IT DOWN!' they all roared.

They plunged their lit torches into the plush velvet seats, the satin drapes, the curtains, the screen, and fled. Within minutes the place was an inferno. Somehow, Billy managed to find his way through the black smoke to the roof outside. Coughing and spluttering, he staggered across the roof's ledge to the canopy at the front of the building, his clothes singed and burning. The infrastructure was perilously unsafe now; bits of masonry already starting to crumble and fall. On that devilishly dark Sunday night, silhouetted against golden flames, fearful tears must have streamed down Billy's face as he stared at the jeering crowd beneath him.

'MONSTER! MONSTER!'

Another earth-quaking detonation announced the imminent downfall of the edifice. Billy took one last look at the mob below—the hatred in their eyes—screaming, raging, throwing their garden implements at him. And in that moment, all he could do was look down in pity.

---

[5] This extract is quoted from Grimshaw's private notes—a completely different version of events from the official report he filed.

'I'm not a monster,' he shouted. 'There are no monsters! Only the ones we make ourselves!' And, with that, surrounded by the roaring furnace, he spread his arms out wide like the wings of an angel and fell down to whatever destiny awaited him.

'GET BACK! GET BACK!' shouted Sgt Grimshaw. 'THIS WHOLE PLACE IS ABOUT TO GO!'

Like a collective gasp, the crowd surged backwards as what remained of the cinema crashed down in a cumulous cloud of dust and smoke. There, from a safe distance, the good townsfolk of Birkenhead watched in awe and satisfaction as the final skeleton girders of the 'Showplace of the North' collapsed—and the soul-cleansing flames rose higher and higher.

As for the remains of Birkenhead's own Dr Frankenstein, Henry Sutton—
They were never found.

Fig. 1

The Town of Checkers

In the town where everyone dresses in black all the buildings
are white. Only swans and crows are allowed to alight.
All the food eaten is black or white. Sloes, olives, grapes.
Potatoes, bread, cheese. Bananas must split from their green

or yellow jackets at the town's breezy limits. *Citizen Kane*
and Woody Allen's *Manhattan* are everyone's favourite movies.
The pattern upon pattern of Disney's *Fantasia* would be
dismissed as mania in the town where only the end

and beginning of *The Wizard of Oz* are known. Nobody
has seen how Dorothy's shoes bled as they shone. When
the sky blurs blue they pray for clouds. Every home is heated
by a special oven which gobbles coal aloud while hiding all

flames deep in its black gusting brain. Snow is the most yearned-for
weather after black hail. Right at the start of life, blonde and red-haired
babies are discarded in baskets on the outskirts of the next village
five rabies-riddled hills away. Chess is the most popular game.

Dice are played too but cards are burnt whenever diamonds or hearts
are thrown. The tarot is unknown so in three-year cycles a travelling nun
arrives and deciphers everyone's palm, dispels their fears, while for weeks
afterwards dreams are wheeling with colours no one has the language to explain.

Patrick Cotter

The Feather

Vladimir Poleganov (translated from the Bulgarian by Peter Bachev)
For Leena Krohn

X,

I've just finished reading your letter and, frankly, I am struggling to make sense of it. Do you really think I would go the lengths of fabricating such a thing just to excuse my absence and lack of contact? You've known me for... how long has it been? Years, decades! Have I ever even attempted to cajole or pacify or confuse you with made-up stories? Have I? Even when a lie could have helped the situation, I've always been honest with you. Yes, I concede, oftentimes, while still in the grip of something I'd recently read, I would enthuse about it to you in a way that is more in line with imagination than recollection, but I've never knowingly chosen a lie where a memory would've done. Never!

My last few letters—five, to be precise—went unanswered and the sixth one... well, it was certainly not the response I'd been hoping for or anticipating (*'Don't you understand how important it is to try not to do that?!'*). Please do accept my apologies if your words have failed to reach me for some reason, but I doubt that's the case—Avinia's postal service enjoys its excellent reputation for a reason and its pigeons are the fastest and most adroit in the world. I therefore assume that your current letter is the first one in quite a long time.

Anyway, what's important is that communication has been reestablished and I can finally talk to you again. I say 'talk'... But letters are not at all like conversations, are they? Of course, they can be long and nurturing and emotional and bring you a little bit closer across the divide, and yet every piece of paper is a symbol, the physical manifestation of loneliness, of the enormous emptiness they've had to travel, of one's absence, of—let's be honest here—the inevitability of death. As we know, every absence or separation is a small death. A letter comprises, by its very nature, all the things conversations, especially ones as intimate as ours used to be, try to sidestep, move on from, forget about and delay and escape. I would like to believe that one day the distance between us will be laughable, no longer an obstacle for any bird, let alone homing pigeons; that an extended hand, mine or yours, will be more than long enough to bridge it, that our words won't have the all that empty space to echo in.

For now, however, we will have to come to peace with the circumstances that have scattered us to the opposite corners of the world. I don't know about you, but my reconciliation sets in gently, almost imperceptibly, because this place is wonderful. My words are bound to disappoint you, I realise, but I can't help but write them: Avinia is where I belong. It is also where I think I'll find the Feather. Remember the Feather? But of course you do! I still haven't managed to identify the bird it came from, there are simply too many of them here—darting through the air, diving down into the ocean or just jumping around—but it is only a matter of time, I can feel the moment finally approaching!

And there I go again, more excited than I really should be if I am to show you that I can indeed think and act responsibly. I shall end my letter here.

Please write back and do not forget about me.

X,

So soon!

When they brought me your letter, I genuinely thought they were mocking me. My friends here take great pleasure in playing small pranks on each other. They would make the victim believe something was happening and then, abruptly, pull the curtain, take off the masks and the letter, for instance, would turn out to be an invitation to clean guano off the Southern Rocks or a map for a moa egg treasure hunt in the thick jungle of the Central Island. But your letter is not a joke, it's real, it didn't send me off somewhere looking for the eggs or bones of ancient birds, but instead lit up my day, as if I'd heard your stories in person. I am excited to see your new home and I'm sure your puppy is adorable! Also, you are wrong, my dear—reading of that old copy of *Birds of the Balkan Peninsula* finally falling apart doesn't make me mad, not even a little—I don't need it anymore! Avinia has every book on birds I could ever want: its library holds, for instance, not only things like the latest article on the dwindling population of the house sparrow in Europe, but rare publications, such as the original manuscript of *De arte venandi cum avibus*, ostensibly lost in the siege of Parma, but actually salvaged for the ages by four of the librarians' carrier falcons. And that's not all: there are so many copies here of *Birds of*

America that if I sold them, I'd be the richest man in the world—and don't get me started on what I saw, touched and felt while reading Attar's *The Conference of the Birds,* it really deserves its own letter... No, not today, I still can't seem to tame the images into anything even resembling a coherent story. I felt like a dead or hibernating tree might feel when the weight of the thousand starlings on its branches makes it believe that spring has come, only to be left behind in their shadow moments later as a sudden sound startles them off into the distance...

Forgive me, here I am again, getting excited and running off on tangents. But let me push the parentheses just a little further apart and tell you about how the Hoopoe of Attar visited me in my dream. He wasn't there for long and barely uttered anything the human ear would recognise, but after he had gone, I slept peacefully: his flock was looking for a whole new God, whereas all I need is to find the body that my Feather belongs to. It's sometimes a relief to be reminded. Anyway... parentheses closed!

You may remember how I never told you I was leaving, to chase after the Feather's original owner, that Feather that I found the last summer day you and I went walking down the promenade. 'Look! What a strange feather,' you said, and then, as I picked it up, 'Isn't it really strange? It looks unreal, almost like it's been drawn by a human hand'. You may remember how, for days after that walk, I would stay silent: you thought I was sad or angry, I was really just speechless—thoughts of the Feather had completely usurped my mind, I could not care about or concentrate on anything else. I spent weeks trying to find the species of bird It could have come from, to no avail. I am sorry for that time I called you up at four in the morning, to complain, to talk to someone, really, about how the unknown— no, the *unknowable* bird's dark silhouette, of which I had only a single bright and clear piece, the Feather, tortured and terrified me, its vortex pulling me into an ever-expanding void, every time I closed my eyes. Here, that silhouette no longer holds power over me. I still see it, perhaps not quite as clearly, in the corner of my eye from time to time, like a diorama of death or a small shadow—a *haze,* rather—of suppressed desire, but it doesn't jump out at me anymore from the depths of my subconscious. It is indifferent to my frantic attempts to pull myself out of its invisible, murderous tide.

Ah, the Bird island... I still don't have the words, I'm afraid, to tell you how I made it to Avinia's shores, maybe they too will come one day. But don't go looking for me, dear, if that's what you're suggesting in your last sentence. Don't go looking for me.

X,

With all due respect, Avinia is a fairly well-known island between India and the Arab peninsula. Even Alexander the Great visited it once and is often quoted saying he would've liked to stay forever because he had fallen in love with a swan. Well, at least the local history books claim it was a swan, it could've been a commonplace tufted duck for all I know, the lakes around here are teeming with them. Napoleon was heard saying he'd 'rather be exiled to Avinia' too... Please excuse the firmness of my tone (I hope the ink softens by the time it reaches you), but do some research, because your last letter's opening paragraph is downright insulting.

I wanted to tell you about this ostrich competition I witnessed, and the invitation I received immediately after to train as an ostrich rider, and about the glow in people's eyes as they assured me I'd have a bright future as one, but I'll leave that for another time. I'm enclosing something instead that was supposed to become a diary of sorts, written for you and you alone, but that ultimately remained a single sheet of paper; a nice memory dried up and framed by words. I don't really feel like writing today, I'm sorry.

The first few days I stayed with a local bird-painter. Old, bald, hunchbacked, he looked like a flat-faced marabou stork. He would scurry about his flat for no obvious reason, rummaging in this or that cupboard or chest, peeking into rooms and behind curtains, as if looking for his missing beak. Power would go out at night—at his request, he later explained, so that he can revel in the complete darkness of the world. 'It is the only way I can truly see the birds,' he would say. 'Nothing looks like its true self in the light of day, everything is polluted: the colours, the lines, everything'. The surprise in my eyes must've been obvious— isn't it contact with light that makes colours and shapes possible in the first place?—so he would smile and explain: 'The images one receives as a dream or a vision, or those impressed upon the underside of one's eyelids by ecstasy or insanity, those are the most beautiful and the clearest of all images—they are like feathers, they fall softly onto the memory, but leave an indelible trace.

'Have a look at any one of my paintings, take a good long look and then close your eyes firmly and try to recall it, flow back to it through the prism of your memory the way light does. It is very different, isn't it? Only then does the painting respond, only then does it talk to you. I have no interest in producing pictures that are mute—so I paint them the way I see them in the darkest depth of my mind, the way they are in the midst of my innermost night.'

X,

I am positive I heard two old ladies talking about you today. I know it sounds improbable, but I swear it is true! I was having a stroll through the Park (the full name of which is as long as it is banal—the Garden of the Feathers That Fell From the Sedge of Cranes And Foretold Sarama Ecka's Future—but the story behind it is really interesting and has little to do with either cranes or Sarama Ecka herself. I'll tell you some other time, for now I will refer to it simply as the Park, the beautiful Park with alleyways powdered with fine grey sand and emerald green pines) when the sharpness of their conversation pierced through the stillness around me. I say pierce because if their words were tangible, they would have darted through the air, clawing and biting and tearing it to pieces, the way swallows and bullets and screams do with the low-hanging summer clouds. Be it because of the animation in their voices, or one's peculiar laughter, however, what I heard when I started paying attention was more of a crackle than a whistle: in fact, they sounded like a pair of magpies, excited by a glimmer in the grass.

One of them was saying: 'X has such a beautiful face, I can't help but wonder why it's fading?' 'It's not fading, it's just drifting further away,' answered the second one. 'You know how it is in other cities around the world, don't you?' 'I know, I know, faces there… They don't *endure*, do they?'

And then I stepped out of range and could no longer hear them. I know it is impossible that they were talking about you, but it *felt* so logical. They were right too: I don't think your face will endure for much longer where you are. I'm not trying to scare or threaten you, I'm just warning you. Your face will fade, will become transparent, like a veil to a void. I'm not sure even your eyes will be able to withstand—they may remain as black and strong as I remember them, able to keep burning the gentle flame that contours your features for a little while, but this world you are stubbornly clinging to, this world will always try to efface you, to make you so weak and thin that it could disassemble you, scatter you like ash or a lingering scent, with a stroke of its hand. Believe me, I know what this world is capable of, it almost happened to me.

X,

This letter will be very short. It should hopefully reach you quickly and not take too much of your time: I have read Leena Krohn, heard of Jan Morris, and am very much aware that there are dozens, maybe hundreds of authors who have written letters from imaginary lands. I understand what you're hinting at, but you're wrong. I also don't think we can communicate in any other way, I am sorry. You're wrong about that too.

X,

I know that the Feather belongs to none of the many different species of owl that call Avinia their home, but for some strange reason I can't stop thinking about them. Do you remember what you wrote that night we stayed up, sleepless, with nothing but the old farmhouse's collapsed roof between us and the dark sky? Here, I know it almost by heart:

The owl is the most silent of birds. In flight, even the air that parts to let her pass doesn't quite realise she is there. The owl can fly through dreams and memories, her shadow does not cloud the eye or weigh on the heart. That's because the owl herself is so light—lighter than the gentlest part of the night and the sweetest hour of the day: a recollection of a dream. The owl's golden gaze is the longest thing on Earth. They claim it stretches from ancient times to the end of days, even beyond. The owl's feathers are the slowest to fall—neither night nor day want to surrender them to gravity, so they rarely ever reach the ground. They say the earth is most thirsty not for water, but for owl feathers. The owl's beak can tear anything apart, especially that which does not belong—flesh or stone—so that order can be restored. They say that if the owl didn't hunt or feed, the world would be thrown off balance—one side will descend into chaos like quicksand, the other float away untethered into nothingness. In the darkest midwinter, when snow has covered flesh and stone alike, the owl feeds on synchronicities. In the height of summer, when even the Earth is clawing its own face off, looking for another pair of lips to taste the sky with, the owl feasts on wishes.

Both wishes and synchronicities abound, but are usually hidden for anyone but the owl. The owl sees everything: flying over, tugging their corners closer together, sewing up the world where it threatens to come undone. It is a difficult, time-consuming task, they say, hence why the largest part of the owl is her tomorrow—a limitless tomorrow, of the kind rarely seen in nature. With a tomorrow that size, one would think the owl's number is eight—infinity upright, a vertical gaze, Siamese suns—but it is not. The number of the owl is five. Because 5% of her weight is concentrated in her eyes (and that's mostly her soul); because five are the eggs she lays in those years when the most wishes come true and synchronicities are the strongest; because five are the colours of her feathers; because five are the directions the owl can fly in: East, West, North, South and towards you.'

It was then, I think, and for a little while after, that you and I were on the brink of discovering this new world we had spent so much time dreaming about, this world we had populated with stories about ordinary animals with extraordinary habits and abilities. But then something pulled us back, just as we were learning to read the map of these new places we suddenly had access to, something yanked the invisible chain around our necks and made us lose the thread. What was it, X? What held us back? These days I can't help but think it was the shadow of that bird, the one my Feather belongs to. I don't believe we actually *found* the Feather that last summer day, I think, careless in our ignorance, I think we *tore* it out… What did you have to notice it for? Had we just walked on, like so many other passersby that day, we would now be in that other world, where owls hunt not mice but wishes and where birds of paradise can no longer fly from all the wonder that sticks to their feathers.

X,

Your last letter made me think of Death. Are you so petrified of it that you've allowed yourself to forget things as important as your writings on the owl? Were you not more afraid of all the empty lines, empty white walls and smooth sand, of all the places one could leave a mark, write a message, tell the truth? Isn't that what you used to say—that you fill them in so you never forget? I spilled a little of your ink just now, I guess I got excited again, but I won't bother starting the letter over. The more I look at the stain, the more I am reminded of the bruises on your skin that night—I couldn't find the right words then, any words, really, as I was leaving, but we both knew (or at least felt, instinctively) that we shouldn't have picked the Feather, or even noticed it. But by then it was already too late—the bird-shaped vortex of darkness had already started spinning.

X,

I'm sending this second letter without waiting for your response, hoping that it catches up with and erases the first one from your memory. I wasn't quite myself writing it. That tends to happen to me occasionally and the ink preserves it like an impatient and inept photographer. But it doesn't matter, really—photographs fade, and I see you too have learned to forget. Forgive me.

There is a graveyard in Avinia, perched upon a hill close to the city, which birds and humans share. Scientists are yet to come up with an explanation, if they're even looking for one still, but this is the place where all birds go to die. Whether they know when Death is about to transpire and circle the hill in waiting, or whether there is something in that particular starry strip of sky that cuts them off from life, is unclear. In any case, during the day, the graveyard is white and shiny, like a Greek village in the midst of summer: tombstones are always polished, the names of the dead carved in stained-glass. The bones of birds are also white, so that when the sun rises, it sets the whole hill alight. I often find myself staring at it, hypnotised by its brilliance, but also hoping, almost half-expecting, to see a phoenix fly out of the incandescent pyre on its skyward way home.

At night, on the other hand, be it due to phosphorus residues or by magic, the graveyard bathes in a light that some may call ghostly, but to me looks more submarine. Whenever I come here after dark, I feel like I've just sunk to the bottom of a crisp mountain lake. I look up at the stars, barely visible through the greenish light haze, and all I see is the eyes of some predator, come to hunt at the watering place. I once met an old woman, an augur, negotiating her way across the overgrown alleyways, looking for small bones suitable for divination. It is an art well-preserved in Avinia and people really believe in it still. I didn't dare ask her anything, even mundane things like whether it is hard to collect enough bones for a whole session, or what birds carry the brightest futures under their feathers and flesh. I just watched her for a while, her feet dancing between the fragile skeletons, collecting the white letters of tomorrow's histories.

X,

I guess I shouldn't be surprised that your answer is running particularly late this time around, especially after that story about the graveyard, but that doesn't mean that days don't drag agonisingly slow or the empty hands of my friends, hands that I had often regarded with suspicion, expecting prank letters but hoping for a real one, are any easier a sight to take in. I remember you saying that I mistake imagination for longing. Everybody makes mistakes, I guess. But if you forget me, it would be a conscious choice, not an inevitability; not the unfortunate symptom of confusing memory and desire, but a decision to regard the two as tantamount to each other. (You used to say that we remember things as they are, not as we want them to be. Yet in my experience, that rarely happens. And remember: the objects of desire are not as constant as desire itself, you used to say that too.) I've been wondering lately if you no longer remembering me is something that has already happened, rather than an impending possibility. I visualise myself reading your past (dragged here against its will, in the form of a stack of old letters or a full notebook, by four nimble carrier falcons, the letters on the page small and faded to mere braille dots), and the moments we've spent together are written in some foreign language I don't understand. Someday, I am sure, you'll tell yourself and your friends that I don't exist, never have. You will laugh and use words like 'fiction' and 'mirage' and 'stupid', or perhaps even 'just a fragment of my dream history'. I don't seriously think you are punishing me, that's not it; I do know, however, that part of your silence is, if not malicious, than at least on purpose. The part that corresponds to your conviction, the belief that you've shared with me, more than once in the midst of a heated argument, that if we don't leave space in our lives for the silence, the emptiness, the inexplicable, they will eventually take over and we will slip into oblivion, paralysed by confusion and terror. I still don't know if I understood you then, if I understand you now. Maybe you really are no longer afraid of empty lines, white walls and smooth sand, maybe you can now erase, rewrite, and rearrange as freely as you want to, wherever you want to, yet I would still rather explain away your unresponsiveness as a lesson of some sort, the same way I used to rationalise the strange gaps in your accounts of everyday life when you still wrote to me. What lesson? Well of course, the one about the End, the one that has always moved and impressed you, the only thing you were ever able to lecture on.

    I can feel the coming winter, it has been in the air for a few days now. The Bird I'm looking for has probably already flown south. Or north. Or back to you. I have no strength left to follow it. The Feather is still here, I can see it from where I'm sat. I don't suppose you remember what it looks like anymore, do you? If asked now, you would probably describe it as belonging to a pigeon or a crow, grey and unremarkable. You wouldn't have noticed it or asked me to pick it up, the way it now is in your mind's eye. Too bad we can't go walking anymore…

I wrote you a few more pages, but then changed my mind and burned most of them before placing the rest into the envelope. These few pages, now nothing but ash or 'wind ink' as they call it here, outlined some of the reasons why I'm never coming back and why, even if I ever did, I wouldn't answer your call if I happen to run into you in our empty room or on the dirty, congested streets of your city. There is a wall between us, X, an invisible and insurmountable wall, and your words will break silently against it, little more than condensation on the other side of a window, and I will never understand them. And even if I were to try to respond from my side of the glass, to use that brief moment of being every circle of breath has to scrawl something, like a simple 'yes', it would look like the ultimate mockery, the ugliest scar, on your side.

I'm sorry, X.

Please write back.

Essay | Short, Sharp Shocks
Bernice M. Murphy

What makes me *want* to be afraid? Why do I yearn for fictional horrors when the daily news provides more than enough real terror to contend with? My personal and professional interest in horror fiction and film often seems unfathomable to those who find the dark side of popular culture profoundly unsettling. If the misleading—if neat—assumption is that the horror writer or director must have some sort of ghoulish or tragic 'origin story' that explains away their fixation upon the genre, then what excuse do I, and my fellow horror fans, have? Why are we determined to engage with a genre explicitly supposed to inspire dread, fear and even disgust?

Most people occasionally revel in the macabre, but few are fanatical devotees like me. There's usually a good audience for the latest high-profile horror release at the cinema, and many people will happily watch the oldies on TV at Halloween to savour the scares and the unconscious camp that saturates many a bygone classic. Stephen King has been one of the most commercially successful writers in the world for more than forty years. Thanks to shows such as *The Walking Dead, American Horror Story* and *Stranger Things*, horror has a foothold in mainstream TV that would have been unthinkable only a decade ago. And whilst HBO's mega-hit *Game of Thrones* is undeniably a work of fantasy, its many scenes of torture, black magic and 'White Walkers' (ice zombies!) remind us that George R.R. Martin was a respected horror writer long before Westeros hit the big time.

Like chickenpox, horror gets you when you're young. My obsession was fostered by the conspiratorial playground exchange of dog-eared paperbacks by Richard Laymon, John Saul and Shaun Hutson. And let's not forget the completely batshit-in-retrospect oeuvre of Virginia Andrews, author of the 'incest is fine if you're in love!' gothic doorstopper *Flowers in the Attic*. The 'best bits'—pages featuring sex or violence, or more daringly, both—were always signposted by faintly greasy fingerprint marks. Even the silliest mass-market horror paperback or grainy VHS recording was granted a sinister cachet by the fact it was not yet meant to be experienced by *us*. 'Unsuitability' gave these experiences a charge that many subsequent, age-appropriate encounters with horror would lack.

My interest in horror verges on the obsessive, and has done so for twenty years. It costs me money, time, wall space (too many books, too many DVD's) and occasionally, sleep. I take pride in seeing the original, foreign-language version long before most people watch the crappy American remake. I follow the review sections of horror magazines and blogs and film festival reports with the greedy eye of a gambling addict perusing the *Racing Post*. I listen to gruesome true-crime podcasts when I run, despite the fact that their focus on female vulnerability to random acts of horrible violence transforms every gloomy woodland path and grimy city alleyway into a site fraught with the spectre of potential ambush. Horror is one of my most diverting preoccupations. Not quite a religion, perhaps, but certainly more than a hobby.

The most disturbing horror novel I have ever read is one I found shoved down the back of a sofa cushion in the late 1980s, hidden there by my poor mother precisely so that I *wouldn't* read it. That, of course, rendered it irresistible. It was a 1973 oddity titled *Let's Go Play at the Adams'*, written by Mendal Johnson, a debut novelist who supposedly died of alcoholism soon after it was published. It's about a group of All-American youngsters who kidnap their painfully nice babysitter—Barbara—tie her to a bed, and gradually torture her to death.

As an Irish child of the 1980s, I failed to appreciate the novel's specifically American portrait of early 1970s moral malaise, even if the quote on the front cover did frame it as a Nixon-era variation on *The Lord of the Flies*. The same blurb also mentioned *The Exorcist*, which I wouldn't read for another few years, and which had been a massive hit just before Johnson's novel was released. However, for all of its still-shocking elements, William Peter Blatty's intensely religious bestseller is a great deal more conventional than Johnson's desolate, entirely secular debut—I would pick a bout of demonic possession over a week with Johnson's sadistic kids-next-door any time. I raced through the novel, but even as I turned the pages, I wished I had left it down the back of the sofa, in the dark with the lint and the old sweet wrappers, where it belonged. For years, I was haunted by memories of the horrific treatment meted out to poor, naïve Barbara, the casual yet calculated cruelty of her cereal-munching, bickering young captors, and, most of all, the matter-of-fact nihilism of the devastating climax.

My own babysitter was a relentlessly good-natured older cousin who let me stay up late because she was too scared to watch late-night Hammer Horror films on her own. The thought of anyone—least of all a gang of youngsters that included children younger than me—subjecting her to acts of sadism was incomprehensible and shocking. Sure, I'd already seen little Damian Thorn deliberately knock his mother over a balcony in *The Omen*, but there was a big difference between the showy, heavily soundtracked violence perpetrated by the pallid-faced, plump-cheeked Antichrist, and the mysteriously empty yet decidedly ordinary youngsters who populated Johnson's novel. Damian was an obviously supernatural figure contained by the framework of a star-studded Hollywood blockbuster. There is no such comforting distance here. Barbara's captors—mockingly self-named 'The Freedom Five'—start the novel by telling themselves that her imprisonment is nothing but a silly prank carried out on a boring summer day. But they soon find that once they have broken, as Johnson puts it, 'the law between children and adults… nothing was happening. They ignored the taboo, and no lightning fell'. They're not mentally ill, or spawns of the Devil, or alien invaders. There is no excuse or explanation at all for their actions, save for the absolute moral vacuum that makes their torture of Barbara possible.

Years later, I found out that *Let's Go Play at the Adams'* was loosely based upon a notorious real-life case: that of Indiana teenager Sylvia Likens, who was tortured to death by her foster mother and a group of neighbourhood kids in 1965. With that realisation, a novel that had long been a distressing mental touchstone was rendered more upsetting, yet, at the same time, more morbidly fascinating. I re-read an old copy: it was as disturbing as I remembered. It was also more obvious that Johnson's treatment of sexual assault was dubious, even by 1970s standards. The ending was still stomach-turning. But this time I went out of my way to recommend it to other horror fans.

It was clear to me now that Johnson was trying to create an effect that horror, at its most uncompromising and challenging, conjures up more successfully than any other genre. His unsparing work is an attempt to look beyond the everyday façade of bourgeois 1970s upper-middle class suburbia, behind the smiling, socialised masks that we all present to the world. Crucially, it's not just the villains who have their inner lives laid bare on the page; Johnson devotes almost as much time to Barbara's self-critical, rapidly evolving interior monologue as he does to the thought processes of her killers. His novel forced me to contemplate the most unpalatable facets of human nature at an age when I was just beginning to appreciate the idea of free will and the existence of 'evil' as a real-world concept that could be perpetrated by otherwise 'normal' people.

Let's Go Play At the Adams' is a blunt tool calibrated to make an obvious point: the kids here are most definitely *not* all right. As such, it has a lot in common with later, better known treatments of the same theme. In a bone-deep way that eludes many of its successors, however, it tries to evoke *true* horror— that unmistakable mix of unease and anxiety that hits you on both a visceral level and, more lastingly, on a philosophical and moral plane. 'Escapist' in the conventional sense of the word it is not, but it is a novel that evokes, through its entirely uncompromising depiction of victimhood and villainy, the ways in which we justify our cruellest impulses to both each other and ourselves.

Let's Go Play at the Adams' was the moment my tipping point was reached, when my relationship with horror went from passing interest to genuine fascination. For me, reading it is like reading the nihilistic short stories of Thomas Ligotti, or watching the nightmarish French masterpiece *Martyrs*; the psychological equivalent of deliberately grabbing an electric fence. The sensation that results is acutely unpleasant, but it is also terribly, unforgettably *real*. Though I have boundless affection for the horror genre in all of its guises, it is, above all else, the prospect of encountering another work that haunts me in the way that Johnson's novel has that keeps me coming back for more. That makes me yearn for that short, sharp shock—and the revelatory dread that follows in its wake.

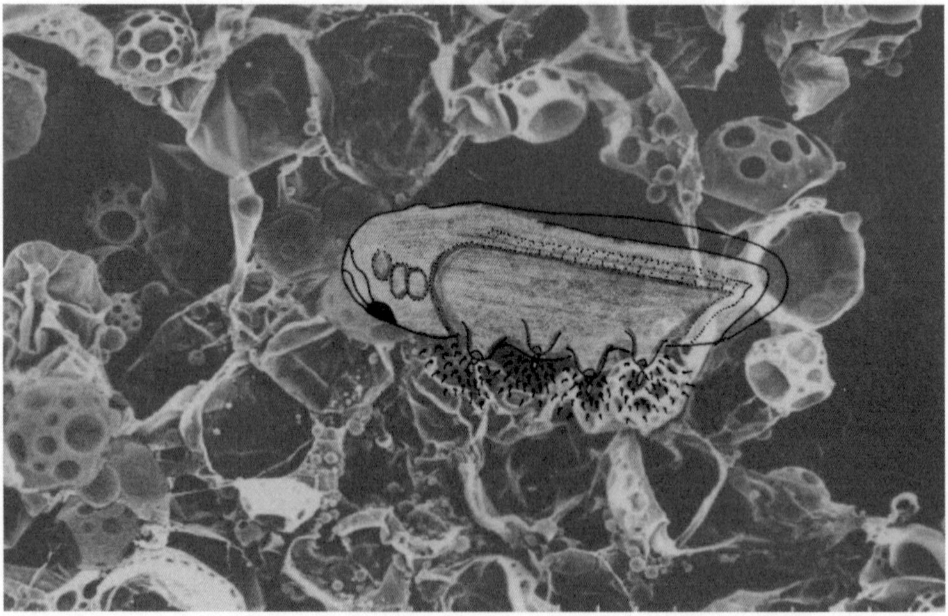

</RECORDING BEGINS>

Dominus vobiscum, brothers and sisters, for today we are **Athanasius contra mundum**.[i]

In *Laudato Si*, published thirty years ago by the heretic cardinal and papal pretender Jorge Mario Bergoglio,[ii] an unhealthy emphasis was placed upon the environment. Yes, the Lord has entrusted the earth to us as his stewards, but nowhere did the Angelic Doctor in his formation of Natural Law state that the good of the earth was to come at the expense of the good of man.

Laudato Si did, however, contain one important kernel of truth, perhaps more relevant today than to the age in which it was written. It said:

> "*The acceptance of our bodies as God's gift is vital...thinking that we enjoy absolute power over our own bodies turns, often subtly, into thinking that we enjoy absolute power over creation.*"[iii]

The Cardinal was correct. We do not enjoy absolute power over our own bodies, nor should we ever feel entitled to exercising absolute power over creation.

We may not stifle the procreative function of the conjugal act.

We may not toy with the very fabric of being and splice human DNA with that of frogs and fish.

Man, as pinnacle of creation, has an inherent dignity and an allocated life-span. When we are called to God, so we go to our rest, there to stay until the Day of Judgement when Christ will come again in glory.

Altering the fundamental substance of our being, undermining the preciousness and uniqueness of human life, is arrogance and evil.

Charles Baudelaire was a sinful and excessive man in life, and yet he repented and turned to the mother Church before death. His summation of the work of Satan is very apt for this moment in which we find ourselves: "*The devil's finest trick is to persuade you that he does not exist.*"

The Devil does exist and his manifestations are clear today in the arrogance, pride and heresy of modern science and even within the previously-sanctified walls of the Vatican. The creation of the monstrous, unnatural creature known as **Xenopthor** has had the direst of implications for man's understanding of our bodies as divinely-

Cute
Ian Shine

I always Photoshop pictures of my girlfriend before I put them on Facebook. I take an outline of her jaw and pull one or two points out of place, or smudge a rhubarb blotch onto her laundry-white skin. Sometimes I drag the mole above her lip into just the wrong place, other times I distort her stomach into a doughy pillow.

I tell her I do it to stop my friends wanting to take her away from me, and she laughs and calls me cute, but she never distorts any pictures of me.

It makes me pretty uncomfortable, having such a beautiful girlfriend. Each time I kiss her pixel-perfect lips I fear it'll be the last. Sometimes I sit up at night and go through the doctored pictures on my phone, thinking things might be better if I had a girl like that, with frizzy hair and a crooked nose, a gap in her teeth or uneven breasts.

She comments on some of the pictures: 'Do you think I look cute?' One day she even posted a picture on my timeline, showing her looking as ugly as a normal person, and I gave it a like. When she came through the door looking exactly like the photo, I fainted. She said the surgery had cost thousands.

I take her out everywhere with me now, and all my friends think she's totally average. Sometimes we spend the evening trying to Photoshop her new face back into her old one, but we always end up laughing too much to manage it. Then she strokes my hooked nose and my bald patch, and says they're cute. I kiss her stubby chin and protruding ears. They could be cuter.

In His Attic

He holds the parcel out to me
and it is my heart,
swaddled in blue tissue.
Cold, white,
quietly convulsing.

*Look! Been saving
this, all these years.
Not a scratch on it.*

Boxes and boxes
behind him—full
of us. Captured.

I've been so careful.
He smiles at the fist
of twitching muscle
in my hands.

It is, indeed,
unbroken.

Susan Millar DuMars

The Boy Who Left
Anne Griffin

We had never really spoken, Fionn Casson and I—unless you count: 'Chemistry is definitely in A3' or: 'Mr Rodgers said he wants to see you in his office' or: 'Here, you dropped this.'

But I did. I counted every small encounter, making a black line on the side of my writing-desk in my bedroom for each one. By the time fifth year came around, we were on one hundred and twenty three. With each stroke I moved towards him, to where I felt we were destined to be, way out beyond those trivial exchanges and the embarrassment of our years.

He was beautiful. Not handsome, not rugged, but beautiful. No blemish or pimple spoiled his skin. The other boys rubbed themselves raw with lotions that promised to unblock every pore. His wolf eyes—clear and blue as the sign hanging over McCaffrey's ice cream parlour—reached deep inside me. When he was near it felt like a whisper tickling my ear or a breath upon my neck.

And then he left—a new town, the teacher said.

A new life, a new me.

I mourned what had never been mine. I locked myself away in my room for days—lying on the bed, blinking tear-clogged eyes at my desk and all that it had promised. I heard my mother pace the landing. When she was still, I imagined her ear pressed against my door. The rise and fall of her muffled phone conversations with Dr Byrne reached me through the floorboards as she wore down her good carpet in the sitting-room below. In time, and to her relief, I yielded to my life again; rising to take my lessons, my exams and four years later, my vows. I married Niall Masterson. A good man. A handsome man. A man with no backbone.

I became the undertaker's daughter-in-law.

Masterson and Son were the undertakers in Ballymore. Gráinne, Niall's mother, ran the show. Her husband, Peter, had himself undergone the full treatment in the mortuary one year before my arrival in the household. No one knew from what he had died and its mystery had consumed the town:

'He was fit as a fiddle.'

'A horse of a man.'

'Not a day sick in his life.'

I had laughed when conversations stretched to dark deeds and potions mixed beyond the velvet curtains.

'Oh come on, Mam, you're saying she poisoned him?'

'You may scoff, Jeanie, but there's something behind those eyes of hers,' my mother said.

Back then, Niall and I were barely anything at all. A couple of dates here and there. One of those flings I had never thought would amount to much but somehow, a year later, it had manifested into a full blown relationship. My loneliness had brought him to me, my belief that true love was a myth made me stay.

The day I first met Gráinne, I stood before her a nervous wreck. The smallness of the town meant that she knew the stock from which I came. My aunt had been in her class at school, but used hang to around with a different crowd.

'She thought herself too grand for the likes of us,' I remembered Chrissie telling me, sitting at our kitchen table, all painted nails and cigarette smoke. 'All I'm saying is I wouldn't trust that one as far as I could throw her.'

Now Niall held my sweating palm as Gráinne sat on her couch, assessing me.

'Isn't she just gorgeous, Mam?' He smiled with pride as I squirmed, embarrassed, by his side.

And in that moment I caught it—the jealous eye falling at my feet, rising slowly to coil over my legs, over my hips, up, until it dug deep within my chest, traversing the broken edges of my heart, gathering up the secret of his unforgotten name before settling sulkily on my face.

'Jeanie, such a pretty name, for one so…'

Gráinne was stunning in her youth, apparently; lads buzzed like flies around her. 'But when she opened her mouth they'd run.' Aunt Chrissie again. 'Oh, she had a tongue on her, alright. Your man was a saint, though, the husband, Peter. A looker too. She cast her spell and stuck her claws in good and tight. The man had no chance.'

Standing in their house that first night, I dared to steal a glance at Gráinne's face and the folds of withered skin, but saw no trace of what she had once been. Over the years that followed, I would witness her delusion as she looked into the hall mirror every day, preening brittle echoes of long ago. In time, I would refuse to even glance at my own reflection there, so sure was I that something of her lingered, clawing at my skin, stealing my youth and my allure.

I married Niall that autumn. And as the leaves fell like confetti on our heads, their colour warming my face, I knew I did not love him as I should.

I moved into the family home. By day I witnessed Gráinne fawn upon her son.

'There's no one quite like my Niall for the bit of embalming. He has them drained as quick as you like, isn't that right, son?'

'Ah, Mam,' he'd say, grinning.

But at night, when we slept, I imagined she sucked the marrow from his bones, and twisted his spine so he hadn't the strength to contradict her or have an original idea of his own.

'Hold on a while there now, Jeanie—move the sofa? Ah no, Mam has always liked it there, she says she can see who's coming a mile off.'

'It's normally a fry on a Thursday, I'm not sure she'd go for Indian.'

'The finances are Mam's department. She's the brains of the operation.'

In the pictures on the grand piano that no one ever played, she was the only person you saw—the others, father and son, seemed faded, only whispers of who they should have been. Thankfully, our wedding photo never made it there, to that, her personal shrine. Instead, it remained in its box, lying unopened on top of the out-of-date missals that lined the bookshelves under the stairs.

Whilst they worked in the adjoining mortuary, I walked the house. Room after mournful room, bereft of any colour, stuffed full of frills and furniture. I was a voyeur passing through, never allowed to touch or to take part.

'Sure, it'll be more trouble than it's worth,' she said. 'You don't know where a thing is in my kitchen. I've been juggling this place and making the dinner all my life, I'll not be stopping now.'

With my place decided, I read in bed. Book after book—the library was in danger of running out of those I had yet to read—and day after day, except for Saturdays. Saturday was my day to smile. I worked in Frayne's chemist. Before I married Niall, I couldn't stand it; after, all that changed. Suddenly the ailments of the town became a wonderful curiosity. I listened well to Mr Frayne who oversaw my counting of the pills. I loved the endless drawers of things I could not pronounce, mysterious tablets with transformative powers.

The *Irish National Formulary* became my book of fascination, I read it cover to cover. Sometimes I was allowed to borrow it, on the condition I dropped it back Monday morning.

'First thing, mind,' Mr Frayne always said, as I pulled the door shut and waved my assurance through the window.

'God, she is such a cow,' my mother would empathise when I stopped at hers on my way home. 'I wish someone would offer to cook *me* a meal. I'd be happy with a slice of toast. Honestly, those brothers of yours—selfish, just like their father.'

Mam always managed to make me feel better, but that changed once I stepped back over Gráinne's threshold.

'Good of you to join us. It must be nice to be a lady of leisure, gallivanting about the town.'

I began to wither. I could feel it in my bones, the gradual wasting. I wondered if I was shrinking. I weighed and measured myself, holding on to the *Formulary* like it was my only protection against her and my growing insanity.

It was the dead that saved me in the end.

'Here, Jeanie?' Niall called up the stairs to me one Friday. 'How are ya with a bit of hairstyling?'

He was desperate, he said. There had been a spate of deaths and, despite Gráinne's insistence that he could manage on his own whilst she attended her Tidy Towns meeting, he had caved under the pressure.

When she returned, she found me elbow-deep in shampooed hair.

'It takes years and years of practice, Niall. We are trained professionals. There are standards. You can't expect her to pick it up just like that.'

But I had.

On Friday mornings when I was allowed to minister to them, Gráinne being out at various appointments, I'd sing as I carefully bathed and dried each limb. Their hair I gently cleansed and brushed. Their skin I moisturised to a shiny hue, carefully massaging every last wrinkle. The make-up I applied with equal care, covering every sign of what had brought them there. And finally the clothes, chosen by those who loved them, left on the chair inside the door—underwear, shirts, suits, dresses, all so perfectly cleaned and pressed, their final expression of love and longing. I held each article reverently, paying homage to that toil.

My work was slow. Niall, so deferential around his mother, would slag me for my diligence. But as people cried over what I had created, he learnt to stop and give my work its due.

'He was never that good-looking when he was alive,' Mrs Drew said when her husband was laid before her.

I brought in business from all around.

'Why, Jeanie, who would have thought you had such talent?' Gráinne said, smiling, her teeth nearly popping out of her head as she read the latest bank statement.

But when the dead started to die in time for my Friday slot, wanting only me and not her to tend them, her joy began to fade.

'If I were you I'd use more rouge.'

'If I were you I'd not use conditioner.'

'If I were you I'd watch my step.' That one under her breath, though my hearing was better than she supposed.

For a while, the tide began to turn, or so it seemed. There was even talk of children. Niall and I laughed with the excitement of it all. But that brief happiness seemed too much for Gráinne to bear. And while my guard was down she sprinkled hatred on our pillows and filled our shoes with darkness so everywhere we walked no light would follow.

'Well, we can't blame Mam for this,' Niall said on the night I held the evidence of our seventeenth barren month in my hand.

'Isn't low sperm count genetic?'

'Christ in heaven, Jeanie, don't be such a bitch.'

'It's this place, Niall, there's something not right. I'm telling you. It's in the walls, and it's creeping into our skins, I know it. I feel it.'

'Maybe it's you, Jeanie. Have you ever thought of that, huh? That it's your madness infecting us? Feck this!' He stormed out, leaving the bedroom and me to my pacing and my hatred.

No child was ever conceived.

My tears swelled and flowed as I continued to tend the bodies, filling them with even more beauty than they had known in life. At wakes, their people whispered and stared in awe at what death had created. I stood at the back of the room, drained, as they filed past.

And then, without warning, Fionn Casson returned. Nine years on, he walked into Masterson Undertakers and back into my life.

'Hi,' he said as I lifted my head from the reception, 'I rang last night and spoke to Niall—Wait… it's Jeanie, right?' His smile was sad but kind. 'I never thought you'd still be here, in the town, I mean. It's Fionn, Fionn Casson, we were in school together?'

My heart began to knock against my chest as I listened to him tell me of his father's death, the illness that had killed him and his wish to be buried in Ballymore. It took all I had not to close my eyes and record his voice forever in my soul.

Niall arrived to shake his hand and take him to the office. As I sat and pretended to work, my eye wandered to the glass divider and to his neck, his jawline, his cheek. I craved him now as much as I had at seventeen. Mentally I drew another line on my old desk: one hundred and twenty -our. And then he turned and caught my eye.

He kissed me three days later, after his father's funeral. We drank each other in. Desperate to reach inside and taste all there was to know. His fingers traced the sadness on my skin. And when they touched my lips he graced me with his future. I swallowed deep and cried into his heaving body. I held on tightly to his hope. Tasting the possibility of escape.

She must have smelt our love in the air long before he came to settle his bill.

'He's such a nice man, Jeanie. So handsome, don't you think?' she said after he left. She was watching me carefully, his cheque still in her hand.

'I hadn't really noticed,' I said, not lifting my head.

'Oh, Jeanie, have you not seen his eyes? If I were only ten years younger. Bewitching.'

'If you say so,' I said, making neat piles of all that I could find on the desk.

'He's quite taken with you.'

A coldness filled the air as I felt her eyes bore into my back.

'Don't treat me like you treat my boy, Jeanie. I'm no fool.'

I cowered where I stood.

'I suppose you think you can just up and go. Is that what the pair of ye are at?'

The question hung between us. Defeated, I sat down on the chair, but still I would not lift my head.

'Believe me, Jeanie,' she said, bending to my ear, 'I'd happily pay your taxi fare to wherever lover boy might want to take you. But I'll not see you break Niall's heart. Watch your step, my girl, or you will regret it.'

I did not breathe until she'd left me there alone. And then a moan, I was not sure at first was mine, cried out long and pitiful into the room. It took all I had not to run after him, to leave right there and then. I should have.

She killed him four days later—a single car crash on the Kilgarry bypass. The coroner could have said whatever he liked, that he was drunk as a lord, or high as a kite, or asleep at the wheel, I did not care. I knew the truth. I knew that she had planted her poison somehow or cast her spell to force his car to swerve. She had taken him from me, and I had let her.

They laid him out before me.

'Such a tragedy, Jeanie, so young, so beautiful, don't you think?' she said, watching me.

When the door closed behind her, I lay on top of his body and cried into his soul. His coldness crept into me, moving through every pore and cell until I was complete. And then I let him go. From somewhere deep inside I found the will to wash and groom the boy who had left me behind.

'Christ, Jeanie, he's like some kind of angel. What do you be washing these lads with?'

Love, I wanted to tell Niall, love. But I could not look him in the eye.

Later, while mother and son slept deeply, I moved about the house and gathered up my life. I left my bags outside her room and entered without a care. My fingers trailed along her bed-frame, touching her dead cells fallen there. From the shelf, her porcelain dolls accused me of the thing I'd yet to do. Her shoes, racked, row after row below, sat ready to pounce. A pillow, that's all I needed. I could see the very one—pink and frilly, discarded at the foot of her bed. I felt its weight. I lit the candle in her windowsill to summon up the spirits, to let them know another of their kind would soon be on her way. And as I stood a moment there, the clouds moved on, letting the moonlight flood the room. It had never shone so brightly. Stepping into its power, I felt him touch me one last time, soft prickles upon my skin, releasing me of all that raged within.

The candle flame was long blown out by the time I left that night. I drove along the moonlit road away from death and out beyond, to all that I would be.

I was your Golem

I did not exist before you brought me
to life, whispering honeyed litanies
until I was yours. You took me
to Prague, drank lattes in *Slavia*,
climbed Petrin Hill, made me laugh
at the name of the Old-New Synagogue.

After our first fight on Národní Street
outside the *Star Beads* jewellery store,
I cried until you clasped a chain
around my neck and we kissed. You swore
you'd never hurt me again, asked me
to move into your place in the suburbs.

You gave me your credit card,
a mobile phone, nice new friends.
Some nights, you'd check my texts
before I went to bed, ask who I'd seen
that day and go quiet when I told you,
lumber to your workshop in the attic.

But I was strong, I didn't need
to tell you every time I left the house,
and I grew to be the best con artist
when the need arose, until you found
a scrap of paper and dialled the digits,
hung up when a man's voice answered.

You chased me upstairs, shrieking
I was muck—spelled out all the things
you'd ever done for me before you broke
the lock, grabbed me by the neck,
plucked the name from out of my mouth
and turned me back to dust.

Simon Lewis

Ramba Runs On Reddened Gears

Of course, he built her to be perfect.
Materials tested in every way
design flaws exposed to the light
flushed out from where they sought to hide on paper
and ruin his design, his triumph, what would
be the making of him, his faultless clockwork

Wife. His quarters were dark, packed with clockwork
debris painting arithmetically-perfect
jaws of shadow perpetually an inch from snapping shut. Things would
not have gone this way
but everything is simpler on paper
and he had barred his doors against the light.

Her arms machined bronze, acid-etched, the metal pounded light
and flat, a chest that rose and fell by steam and clockwork
too small to see. Work replaced sleep, a muscle ticking beneath his sand-paper
cheek—she had to be perfect.
Her face was a radiant golden mask. She would never smile in any way
but how he had shaped her. He would

trace that smile with a finger, would
lay down tools to cup a cool cheek, light
as the tremoring wing of a bird. And when he tried every way
he knew to bring life to limb, to bring clockwork
to love—Stillness. Perfect
in how little it cared for his tears blotching paper,

the plans he had drawn. His lab became a wasteland, paper-
strewn, jaws creaking closure, why would
she not *move?* Everything had been done right. She was perfect.
Unmoving. Cold. The only warmth the candle-light.
Of course, he had miscalculated. There is no love in clockwork.
Just teeth. The purring way

of steam. They say he saw no other way,
not in the face of that stillness. He opened his wrists, like paper
parting, on the clockwork
teeth of her chest, a final gesture that would
have warmed the heart of any human girl. He'd named her 'Rambda', for the light
he'd barred away, and in all respects, his design had been perfect.

A Museum of clockwork curiosities bought the girl so that her maker would
in some way be remembered until the night she disappeared, naught left behind but her paper-
thin mask. His name had not been light on her: only by her own design would she be perfect.

Dave Rudden

There is a Risk of Decay

There's a long room that is used only for storage and pacing. When I say pacing, I mean walking up and down. It's perfect for that.

He had some enjoyment in going through stuff that ended up in the room. Deciding what to dispose of satisfied him. The kept things slice space inside the room and block paths of draughts. They would fill a dictionary definition with filler words, if this particular room in this particular house were to have a dictionary definition and if the things were to be words.

There'll be some problems with the placement of what is kept, but he plans for that.

Every day the tapping of a stick held by a blind man can be heard from the long room. The dragging and pushing of leggy objects inside the room can be heard from way down the road.

There's a burial space booked, a deposit paid, for every kept object and the sound each one creates. Until his death, he'll be overdrawn and busy deciding on what to keep.

If a stranger sees the room or the objects inside it, there is a risk of decay. Solid materials become almost immediately furry and useless.

On a particularly still day, Lloyd, who owns the house, walked around with a long head. He spoke to strangers and he frightened them. Once he spoke to enough people the room's length shortened, but it looked better. It looked less scary now.

Jennie Taylor

For Silence
Darragh Cotter

When it finally happened we had been predicting it for so long, gossiping about it, guessing about it, passing judgement on it, parsing it out in morsels of hilarious misery that we didn't really care about it anymore. A Whatsapp message to the group:

☹☹☹*he broke off the engagement!!!* ☠☠☠

Cue a shrugging of shoulders and the odd eye roll of *at last, it's finally happened*, allied with a *hmmm* and a mulling over of how appropriate it would be to send a meme of a shocked owl saying *'o rly?'* in response. Of course we felt bad for her—who wouldn't? We didn't know all the details yet but we knew they'd be delicious. And we were excited to hear them, in all their gore. Yet there was almost disappointment, too, now that their relationship had finally spiralled out. What the fuck would we, the dregs of the arts graduates of Limerick, a feckless bitter bunch steeped in laziness and discarded dreams, talk about now? When gathered for coffee, tea or pints we'd always known if there was a lull in conversation, we could simply say:

—Did you hear what Liam did now?

And all heads would swivel towards the source of the question, ears cocked, eyes narrowed:

—No... do go on.

Half the time we had already witnessed the slight, told the others about it, chewed it over and hawked it out, making it even more salacious than it had been in reality. But where's the fun in reality?

What had this Liam done, you might ask, to deserve our boundless opprobrium?

Get comfortable:

1. He's English. Ok, ok, ok, calm down. This wasn't why we disliked him

but you do need to be aware of this because it explains things a little better. English and a third generation soldier.

2. He made repeated racist remarks about the Irish. Micks, thick as shit Paddies, statements like 'I'll Bloody Sunday you', 'Cromwell had the right idea'—these kind of statements were posted on Jessie's Facebook page on a weekly basis. (The English soldier thing makes more sense now, doesn't it?)

3. He broke up with Jessie the night before she was due to visit him in England for a week as he and his army buddies had initiated a slut phase before he went to Afghanistan. *Slut phase* is his phrase, not ours.

4. When Jessie booked a boozy holiday with her schoolfriends for an ostensibly similar purpose, he called her a slut and tried to stop her from going. She still went, but after some light questioning we discovered she had declined numerous offers of meaningless sex during it, because she felt she would have been unfaithful to Liam.

5. When they inevitably got back together after *his* slut phase, he gave her chlamydia. She found out while sorting through their laundry after a phone call from the clinic. She packed her bags, sat on the kerb outside their flat and dialled his number instead of a taxi. The phone rang. He picked up.

Jessie (through choking sobs): You, you, you, you gave me chlamydia. Fucking chlamydia.
Liam: What?
Jessie: CHLAMYDIA!
Liam: Fuck sake, don't shout.
Jessie: Fuck sake, fuck you. I'm leaving. I'm outside and my bags are packed, I'm ready to go.
Liam: Calm down, Garth Brooks, it's not that big a deal.
Jessie: What?... it's fucking John Denver you idiot!
Liam: *If it really was me* that gave you chlamydia I got it during my slut phase, I never cheated on you and it isn't that big a deal, can't you just get some antibiotics and take them, stop being such a bitch about it. Ugh, I've to get checked out too now.

The proposal story is too good to be shoehorned into a listicle. I was doing a course with Jessie at the time, so I got to witness this one unfold it all its glory. It was coming up to Christmas and he lobbed the question at her over a text: 'wats ur ring size?' 'it's not 4 a proposal,' was the text that followed immediately afterwards. He was about to be deployed to Afghanistan, it was definitely for a fucking proposal—I'm going to tell you something and because of the cackhandedness of the proposal it will stretch the bounds of your credulity, but believe me, it is true: he was in Military Intelligence. His job was collecting information, conspiring in subterfuge and making intelligent decisions and *that* was how he proposed.

Jessie went off and got her ring sized in a fancy-looking jewellers while I stood outside on the phone to another friend, providing a live feed. We had taken to openly mocking their relationship at this stage in the hope that she would knock it on the head and tell him to fuck off. Peeved at the constant scorn, Jessie stormed ahead when she exited the jewellers and I tottered after her, describing her angry duck gait down the phone. When I caught up with her, she was on the phone to himself. She hung up.

—What's up? I asked.

—Nothing... He's not getting me a ring anymore. He's getting me something different for Christmas.

—Did he still ask for your ring size?

—Yes.

—I think that's what they call misdirection in the Military Intelligence community.

Oh, we howled at that one.

Lists are reductive, anecdotes are reductive, we know this, we know that this is not a true or complete portrayal of their relationship. And their relationship must have been alright, or possibly even good, at some stage. Maybe some nights when she came home tired and depressed from her shitty job he cooked dinner and cleaned up afterwards without being asked, maybe she rubbed his back as they lay in bed talking about what they would name their children, maybe when they couldn't sleep and it was so dark they couldn't see each other, they talked about the dreams they had that were so ambitious they were ashamed of them. Maybe all these things happened. And who are we to pass judgement on what their relationship was? We were her friends. This is what friends do. Your friends are judging you, they are gossiping about you, they are bitching about you, they are competing with you. You think they're not? You're lying to yourself. But *I* don't do that, you say. That's because you're winning or, worse yet, you think you're so much better, more intelligent, more articulate, more successful than your friends that it's not even a competition. Friendship is solace, but it is also a contest, and Jessie was losing. She wanted achievements she could show people—but not jobs or money, not houses or cars, no, this was marriage and baby territory. Two kids by thirty territory, stay at home mum territory. And there's nothing wrong with wanting those things, and only those things, until you begin to compromise yourself completely, to parcel up your self-respect and hand it over to a racist, misogynistic fucktard to get a shitty bended-knee proposal.

We did what we did because we wanted to help her. Remember that.

WHATSAPP GROUP: Artsing About

Cara: They put me in charge of the internet today. ☺☺

Nicky: …go on.

Cara: Well, I'm in charge of dealing with customers on Facebook and the Twitter now.

Nicky: The Twitter?

Cara: Yup. I'm really excited about it. Less time on the shop floor.

Aisling: That's great, Cara. Congrats!!!

Cara: Thanks.

Nicky: You getting any extra money for it?

Cara: Not really.

Nicky: Coming down to Limerick soon?

Cara: We'll see. I've got to go home first.

Mary: Woke up this morning with scabby knees and a head like a bag of spiders.

Aaron: Giving blowies out round the back of Costello's again? 8=====D<:o

Jessie: He's started going out with some child.

Nicky: Where'd you go?

Mary: Costello's. I just need to be held.

Aaron: Mess.

Nicky: Want to meet up for coffee? Food?

Mary: Maybe.

Aaron: Where were ye thinking of?

Jessie: She's just turned eighteen. She rides horses. I'm going to tell his parents their son is a kiddy fiddler. 💣 lol…

108 Darragh Cotter

Nicky: You should do that. In person. Just turn up at their door.

Cara: Fuck him. You should block him on Facebook.

Jessie: I'll send you her Instagram.

Aaron: Please do, we'd all love to see it.

Mary: Costa for coffee and then lunch in Napoli? I'm not drinking.

Nicky: Coolness. Meet you there in half an hour.

Mary: Yeah.

Aaron: I'll meet you in Napoli.

Jessie: Instagram account.

Jessie: Fucking slut.

Jessie: Guess he has his skinny girlfriend now.

Jessie: It was my fault though. He always told me eleven stone was the cut-off point.

Mary: Huh?

Jessie: That was his rule. I knew he'd break up with me. My own fault.

Aaron: There was a cut-off weight in your relationship? What a rollercoaster.

Nicky: Lololol

Nicky: You should see the photos on her Twitter. Some ride.

Jessie: She has a Twitter account? Send it on.

Nicky: I don't know if I should.

Jessie: Send it.

Nicky: I'm fucking with you, I don't have her Twitter up, the kiddies these days use Snapchat. Stop bloody talking to him. Have you blocked him yet?

Jessie: How do I screenshot something?

Nicky: Ask Cara, she's in charge of the internet.

Jessie: He called me a psycho bitch and then deleted his Facebook.

Aaron: No he didn't.

Jessie: Yeah he did. I can't click on it.

Aaron: I'm on it now. He's after blocking you… smdh.

Cara: He's an asshole, Jessie. You're better off without him.

Nicky: He blocked you before you could block him? Liam 1, Jessie 0.

Jessie: I hope he gives her chlamydia.

For Silence 109

Aaron: Too.

Aaron: You hope he gives her chlamydia too.

Jessie: I'm going to call his mother. Tell her what her son is like.

Cara: You shouldn't do that. Just forget about him.

The WhatsApp conversations continued for weeks, then months; other smaller groups were set up, none including Jessie. We convened at Mary's flat to discuss how best to address the situation. Of us all, she was the one who'd most recently been visited by an acrimonious break-up, so we listened to her begrudgingly, like you listen to advice about where to go on a holiday from someone who's been there before you. It was a Sunday and those of us still luxuriating on the dole were living on the porridge and hummus left in our fridges after a weekend of mild to deliciously irresponsible debauchery. Gathered around her coffee-table, drinking tins of Karpackie and Dutch Gold and smoking fags, we decided on Jessie's treatment:

—She just needs to get laid.

—I'm not sure that would help.

—Plus it would probably be a little difficult. Have you seen the cut of her recently?

—Well, we need to do something.

—Do we? She has a family.

—Sherrah, they're fucking useless.

—Her sisters told her to lose the weight.

—She's put on a sight of condition alright. It wouldn't hurt to cut the legs out from the table awhile.

—She needs to stop on about him, to forget about him. We can't listen to that shit for much longer.

—It's not like we haven't dropped enough hints telling her to shut up about it.

—She crashed my lunch with Audrey last Friday. I hadn't seen Audrey since Christmas. We couldn't get a word in edgeways.

—How's Audrey?

—I haven't a notion. She followed the two of us around Brown Thomas and Debenhams talking about what to do with her engagement ring. She's still wearing the bloody thing.

—Are you fucking kidding me?

—She told me she's buying a ticket to go over and see him next Tuesday when she gets her dole.

—What? She owes me fifty euro.
—You won't see that again.
—For fuck sake. Lads, this is a pure balls altogether.

It came to a stage where we would groan when *Jessie is typing…* flashed on screen. What conversation would she hijack to moan about Liam, or worse, would she ask to meet up for a drink, would she want to come on a night out and surreptitiously pose with her naked ring finger in sight of the camera, the only thing more obvious than her tumbling neckline? Any and all conversations had to be about Liam, had to be about his latest duplicity, her mushrooming irrationality. We were exhausted. We decided to do what any good friends would do. We silenced her.

It was easy to lure her there; we just started talking directly to her instead of around her. Someone even asked her a question about Liam, God bless that brave fucker. We suggested a night out, some cans before the pub, some dancing before heading to Chicken Hut for some indecent chips with gravy and, though it took some arm-twisting and some cajoling on our part, she acquiesced.

She arrived over in a dress that was, frankly, obscene. Eyebrows hit ceilings, glances shot out the corners of our eyes.

—The state of that cleavage, we muttered out the sides of our mouths.
—You'd lose a small child down there, we said.

Her desperation for attention was heightened by the dress, its caterwauling, its imploring *please stare at me, talk to me, leer at me, its any attention would do* statement. Witnessing her pitiable state, we almost wavered in our task—anyone would've—but we knew how important it was to stay the course. It was for her own good.

In the end, we panicked, didn't even let her finish her first drink. She sat down at the table, tugged her dress both up and down in a forlorn attempt to salvage some modesty. We grabbed a bottle of Huzzar by the neck and womped her in the back of the head. The goose-pimpled base of the bottle met the crown of her skull and she tumbled forward, bellyflopping onto the boozesticky carpet. Miraculously, the bottle stayed intact. We passed it around, examining it, remarking that we had expected it to shatter but here it shone, unbroken, the only spoor of our intervention the wispy hairs and blood matted on its base. Jessie had gone down heavily and some of us were tempted to make a joke about how maybe Liam was right, she was carrying a bit of timber, but this was a sombre occasion so we refrained. We slugged from our cans and began. As we threaded the needle, we remembered nights out with Jessie, walking around Limerick with her at two in the morning, snow drifting down around us, her making a photo album of us studying in Poland and us thinking no one other than our mothers had ever gone to this much effort for us. The needle was Robert Downey Jnr. sharp and we expected it to just slide through her lips but we had to press hard to pierce her flesh. It didn't pop, air did not whoosh through; it just bled slowly as we worked. The criss-cross of the black thread stitching her mouth shut was taut—it would do the job. If we're being honest, we were quite proud of our efforts; we thought it looked artistic, or maybe artisanal. We took a selfie with her before she woke up and made it the picture for the Whatsapp group.

When she woke she was panicked at first, but soon calmed down. That was the first test of the stitches and they held fast. This pleased us. We were surprised at how long it took us to convince her it was for the best, there's only so much patience you can have for a friend's whingeing, the thing with Liam had been months at this stage, and still she'd kept carping on about it. In the end, though, she saw how this would help her; she even let us have her phone so she couldn't message us about it. She was ready to make more of an effort, ready to be a better friend, a better person. We told her she could take the thread out after a month, Mary had read that's how long it takes to develop a habit.

The stitches had unexpected benefits. The weight fell off her, lads on nights out would be burning the ear off her and she'd nod and smile and they'd insist she'd take their number at the end of the night. Her parents bought her a car for being such a trouper during it all. We even gave her back her phone earlier than we'd planned to show what generous magnanimous friends we were.

After the month was up, we approached her with a gleaming scissors, but she shooed us away. She had a new boyfriend from Donegal, her boss kept telling her how pleasant she had been at work lately and that she might even be in line for a promotion soon. She wanted the stitches now, she'd become used to them, their reassuring pressure when she was about to speak. She thanked us for putting them in. She took her phone out and typed a message. Our phones vibrated.

WHATSAPP GROUP: Artsing About

Jessie: I know what's expected of me now.

Creep

the rain falls on Ashfield Gardens
with faded dedication
as you creep to the shop for bread
without money for bread

and in your anxiety
you might hardly have noticed
the boy in the entry
briskly cutting
                his
                             wrist
with the wild orange-paper blade
of a broken Fanta bottle

but you do
and you pause—

he will tell as he saws
as his hand beats to a blur—

that some boy cut himself
by accident
and wiped the
blood

on him
so he needs
blood

of his own
to wipe
on the other boy
to get
him

back

Dawn Watson

Mixed Media

It was in the reception room, on the left as you came into the white room—the painting with spikes, by Brother Benedict Tully. There was a wood whorl, it seemed an eye, near the spikes, so that they could have been a beak. The spikes were blunt, but if you pressed hard enough, you could draw blood. I often ran my hand along them and said I wanted that. He said, 'Yes! Oh, now, I love the wildness of it.'

After walking across the reception area with me behind him, intoning things like, 'Yes. Thank you, Father,' once he had closed the door behind us, his face changed, his robe making a sweeping sound as he gathered speed, rushing me against the wall between the slit windows, where the other monks were passing. I stood as he knelt. I looked at the painting, disappearing into its eye.

David McLoghlin

Just What's For You, You'll Get It
James B.L. Hollands

All around the world, the gays are dancing to Adeva. 'It Shoulda Been Me' is a cover of Yvonne Fair's hit single, itself a cover of Gladys Knight's version, itself a cover of Kim Weston's original, written by Norman Westfield. Hell is a labyrinth.

Adeva's cover is awful, but the gays like it because it's faux-house, and all they play in this place is faux-house. It's miserable. Suits me. No one else seems bothered; they'll dance to anything. They're having a billboard time. The L.A. isn't a bad gay bar in early-nineties London—in fact, it's one of the best.

But the music sucks.

The Angel of Death is sitting just beyond this dancefloor, on top of one of the speakers, reading Sylvia Plath with a torch. He sighs, and makes the black cloud above his head trickle, catching a little bitter rain on his tongue. Pretty bad vibe corner. It's not easy, you know, walking around being the Angel of Death; having to style out not enjoying being the witness to life, finding obtuse ways of merriment that tickle only on the inside. Smiling Reaper: ruined symbol.

I get bored easily.

Now, sick of being ignored, I start to amuse myself by giving people bad trips; watching their bug-eyed, gurning, rushing faces slide and melt as I taps em on the shoulder, and hands em one of my special Tarot cards.

They aren't actually Tarot; they're a pack of baseball cards bought from Little Rickie's on East 4th and First, but they're still the stuff of divination for us. Cards with pictures on them, of the famous freaks from the carnies: Chang and Eng the Siamese Twins, Jo-Jo the Dog-Faced Boy. Photos taken by Charles Eisenmann of people with deformities that the cunt P.T. Barnum used to exhibit for his profit. Our personal Tarot, our friends, mutants of all shapes and sizes, exploited for society's gain. We sit in wait downstairs, a Gordian knot tightening to the muzak of the queers, until the punters are starting to really rush from their pills, then whiplash onto the dancefloor, tap one of the little wuvs on their back and shove a card in their face, in front of their eyes, and whisper, too close to their ear, 'That's you, that is.' Then we step back and watch whilst their little looks of excitement at being witnessed turn to horror as they become the deformity they glimpse on the card and the freak enters their high, to eternally circle round this trip and, perhaps, if I done it right, all their subsequent ones.

As it bums out their mellow, the freaks are freed.

Back in bad vibe corner, we're relaxing with a pint, watching the last queer we freaked crying and being comforted by two of their friends—'You're not a freak, dear, you're not a freak'—when a clone comes and sits next to us. Except he's too young to be a clone and all the clones died in the 80s. But since he's there, and he certainly looks cunted, Death taps him on the shoulder and hands him his card—Koo-Koo, the Bird Girl, a brain-damaged woman who was made to wear a feathered outfit and bite the heads off live chickens for the audience's amusement. This guy just looks at it and laughs. Really laughs.

Dammit.

A cursory intro—Hi. James. Hi. Phil—later and the eyes meet and it's on. This one's a bit thin—not AIDSy thin, just thin, which isn't what we'd normally do, we prefers a bit more bounce to the ounce—but it's on and we snogging, which is OK, but only semi material. It's not gonna be the ride of a lifetime though that could be the speed, so snog and nightbus and soon we're on the route back to Phil's place on the Holloway Road. It's an old fire station turned into a co-op by Circle 33. Zero 33. Their slogan is *Enhancing Life Chances*.

'Nice jacket,' says Phil.

And as we talk about the wings on my leathery back, we tell Phil that they've been painted by a guy called Crusty Chris who's squatting the Bakery, and Phil goes:

'Oh, wait, the Bakery?'

Then: 'Between Clapham North and Brixton, right?'

There's a moment of super-instant distrust—and it's about to bloom into a nebula of full-blown paranoia, which Phil reads superbly, and just carries on the conversation, like that ill wind never blew, to ask if Chris has long dreads, and we're all like:

'Yeah, long dreads, bit full on, never takes his boots off, has to burn his laces off when he does.'

Before we can notice what's happened, Phil is laughing, really laughing.

'Hahahahahahah,' says Phil. 'Hahahahahahahaha.'

Phil's still laughing as he says: 'I'm his uncle.'

Hahahahahahahahahahahahahahahahahahahahahahahahahahahaha.

Then, don't we all just laugh out a hysteria of coincidence, but that could be Phil's excellent grass.

'Hahahaha yes, you're right, Chris *is* a bit full on,' says Phil.

Then: 'D'y'know why?'

Nope, we don't. We don't ask questions, we just blether on a story of our life which is becoming increasingly unbelievable to everyone, including ourselves. Chris, from where we sit, is a live wire. An expert snake, and, like a lot of the squatters, chaos—an avoidance mechanism. Toothpaste on the lovebites of life.

And, this fine day, we find out that the reason Chris is like he is—which is a brilliant, super-scurrying squatter, but fucking full on and borderline not nice—is Chris's father: Phil's brother. Chris's-father-and-Phil's-brother abused both of them; vicious abuse of the highest order. The guy was a monster, not the good kind. This guy tortured and sexually abused both his brother and his son.

Phil seems happy saying this to a stranger, albeit one who knows his nephew, which almost makes us one of the family—shudder—and he says all this perfunctorily, without the trembled lip of the ones who still struggle with flashbacks.

Phil's bedroom is painted with sigils. We're like, you should be careful of all that. We're like, watch that chaos magic. He laughs again. Loud. His laughter really blurts when it comes out, bit too jittery, but strong.

We start the kissing thing as a prelim to the old jig-jag but something's not clicking and it's gonna be peripheral sex. We're a bit twitched though, so, after a half-hearted snog, we redirect to another cigarette (sorry) and then it turns out that the thing at the periphery that's hanging around—wanting an in—is strangulation.

Phil's a bit heavy.

Fair enough, we think. Not our thing, but we're all real decent people, aren't we, and so we don't even think to ask whether he's like, y'know, Strangle Top or Strangle Bottom; we just presume and give his neck a bit of squeeze as he jazzes. Not our bag of spanners.

During the post-coital joint, it turns out that we totally misread the scene and Phil is like, Boss Strangle or a Throat Top or whatever. Not sure what to call him, not having done the Throat Thing before, and it feels like it would be rude to aks him what he calls himself, this Breath Master, this Neck Daddy, just in case he's like a total tard gay Dr Who fan and he calls himself Thaaarg.

But everyone likes an erudite pervert, so we're all hepped up as he's rolling the next joint (please) and laying it down for us that, for him, Uncle Phil, his ultimate sexual fantasy would be if someone came to him as a willing victim. It would be someone who wanted to die, and Phil and the guy would realise each other's fantasies. The guy would be all like, 'Kill me, Phil, kill me, I want it, I want to die,' and Phil would be all like, 'Oh god, I'm going to kill you. I'm killing you. I'm fucking killing you. Oh god, I'm fucking killing you now.'

Or however death scenes go down.

It's really late by now, but cos of the days being up and booze, and Death and knowledge of Death and desire for Death which just suck the life out of one, it's so exhausting, and we know that when we crash, we're really gonna crash, and even though Phil reassures us:

'I won't murder you unless you want me to.'

We're all like: 'I think I'm gonna hafta take a raincheck on that one, bubba.'

And Phil has to get up for work anyway and there ain't no way we're getting up tomorrow, so it all works out, and before leaving, Phil says:

'I'm doing a performance tomorrow, would you like to come?'

And we're like: 'If we're conscious.'

And then: 'Really probably shouldn't say that in front of you.'

The performance is a bit Thaaarg, to be honest, if Thaaarg can be another name for Satan. It's always fascinating watching someone give themselves to Satan. One minute, you're drinking beer and listening to Adeva; the next, you're watching someone you just got off with perform a ritual onstage in front of a large crowd, and he's definitely, definitely, pledging his soul to Satan in return for something or other. It's hard to tell, but we're pretty sure Phil is clear about what he wants, even if it's not translating too well. That's why people practise regular rituals. They're the Powerpoint presentations of the occult.

Phil appears to be dedicating his life to the service of a, or The, Throat God, which we presume is Satan. We're not sure if everyone else in the building is quite getting that Phil really is doing this, it's not a performance like Marisa has just done, where she cracks eggs with her vagina as a symbolic thing. Phil is really doing it. It's not symbolic. Phil appears to want this thing to speak through his own mouth, and is speaking to himself, and then it's speaking through him, in a kinda-not-very-good death metal voice, which is probably exactly how Satan speaks.

Bit camper than he actually thinks he is.

See, Phil appears to want someone else to speak through his own mouth. He's trying to be possessed, or maybe he is possessed and is showing it in public, or maybe he just wants a new language other than the one he's been given, other than the language of abuser and victim. Phil appears to be asking The Throat God to take his soul if he can only strangle someone to death. The audience are the witnesses. Everyone needs a witness.

If each part of reality is represented by a symbol, then language is a model of reality. This is the essence of Ludwig Wittgenstein's philosophy. It is also the essence of magic. Just saying it could even make it happen.

There's a subtle change in air pressure during Phil's performance.

We're quite impressed.

The whole event is something to do with the Sex Maniacs Ball and we go backstage and Tuppy Owens is there talking about how much she likes getting fucked in the arse by builders, and Jona Lewie walks past, and we are sitting on the floor waiting for Phil to come out of the dressing room area and, as Jona Lewie walks past, we kick him in the shins, making it seem like an accident. That's for 'Stop The Cavalry'. Wanker. Jean-Paul Gaultier is there and our oldest friend Andrea is just about to push him down the stairs when Phil comes out of the dressing room and he's really pleased to see us and we fuck his throat really hard in one of the toilets. We leave, looking at paintings without knowing the history of art.

It's so hard to tell what people want.

We get to know each other well, Phil and me. Phil explains his philosophy of life—that everything is written under the sun, we just have to work out the words; how to read. Phil believes that if you just work out the correct order of things, you will know what's coming to you. Just saying it could even make it happen.

We're dubious.

Phil says that it has no choice; that the universe has no choice in these matters. Phil says that the universe has no choice, and you don't, either. It's just a matter of hearing that which is underlying, which is what makes people afraid. None of us *reaaally* wants to know what the universe has in store for us. Phil says you just have to listen harder, to hear your way, listen to what you should be doing. Everything is inevitable. If you listen, you'll know what's coming for you. If you know what's coming for you, you'll be prepared, and if you are prepared for eventualities, you can alter them. But you'll always get what's for you in the end.

We aks him, kinda therefore, why he does invocations and magic if what he's going to get will happen to him anyway?

He says time is relative.

Even though he's a civil servant, and civil servants are creepy, Phil's a laugh to hang around. We play games with him—we let him make a death mask of us, face, eyes and mouth covered with bandages, straws in our nostrils. We know he's masturbating as we sit there, blind, feeling the wet, musty plaster of Paris harden over our face. It seems like a nice thing to do for a friend.

Phil is an expert in music. He teaches us about the different periods in classical music, and he gets a puppy and calls it Spunk because he likes shouting 'Spunk! Spunk! Spunk!' when they are out walking on Finsbury Park. Some people externalise their voice through their pets.

What Phil is into is the idea that murder is the base note of humanity. He thinks that murder, the first murder, the primal murder, don't murder for food, murder for fun, created consciousness in turning the universe's universal Yes to a No. He thinks that murder is the first work of art and that all art aspires to the condition of magic. By working out how complex classical music forms are composed, he creates new pathways in his brain. And if his will is capable of neurogenesis like that through just listening to structures in music, then imagine what murder could do. He thinks that murder will burn such new synaptic paths in his hippocampus that he will be able to find his way out of the maze that was made for him when his brother abused him. It's sacrifice of himself via another willing victim. Ethical murder. He wants renewal, like a soul transplant, like turning the big No he had as a child into a big Yes, and the sound of the universe breathing is Yes, so he'll turn that into a No: renewal forever.

Phil's a vegan.

I was never abused as a child, I don't really know how to judge his thoughts, or if I can, or if I should. I don't have the correct frame of reference. I don't have an objection to death, obviously, like the Angel of Death could have, or maybe I could, but I can't find any ethical argument against Phil's logic. If I think euthanasia is correct, then I should think his desire is too. I guess.

The Angel of Death. He's not really the Angel of Death. He just walks around, pretending to be, to get over the amount of people dying around me. He's so omnipresent, it's like he's metastasised our personalities.

So you may as well glamorise the content.

*

We lose touch with Phil after a while, rivers become streams, then he rings up a coupla years later, out of the blue, asking us to come round to his flat because he has a business offer he'd like to make us, he wants us to go into business with him on a computer program which helps learning for O Levels. The Angel of Death is hardly business partner material, and we know next to nothing about teaching, but we do know about the inevitability of consequence—and so we go and we sit and we have Earl Grey tea, black, no milk, no sugar, and we listen to Debussy whilst discussing his plan.

'Oh wait, I've got something to show you,' says Phil, and we go out of his flat to one of the stairwells. It being an old fire station, the stairwells are completely sealed off, and there are fire doors in-between the corridors, creating air locks. *Enhancing Life Chances*.

We go down to the second floor. There's a large, maybe eight or nine foot long, scorch mark, blackened onto the landing of one of the staircases.

The word immolation is from the Latin *immolare*, to sacrifice.

Everyone needs a witness.

    'Look,' says Phil.
    'There's been another fire.'

Milltown Cemetery, Belfast, March 16th, 1988

The last of the three coffins had just been lowered
when the first grenade exploded. I was blown
twelve feet away, yet landed on my back unhurt.

Over the PA a voice called out to get down.
The crowd of mourners and journalists broke up
in panic, scattering like debris. Some were
gathering themselves from grave-plots—
underwater knells booming in the deep of their heads.

A woman was carried past, her head covered in blood.
Another grenade exploded. Pistol shots rang out
and an overweight man, with black fuzzy hair
and a thin beard, appeared out in front of the crowd,
holding a nine-millimetre Browning pistol in his right hand.

He then raised both hands triumphantly up into the air,
one fisted, one bepistolled, inciting the crowd to *come on*—
his mouth, muted by the din, fish-gasped inaudible insults
as he produced another grenade and lobbed it into the air.

The sea of people parted as it sank and the dull sound
of the explosion lifted a cloud of dust into the overcast sky.
Film crews lay spread-eagled behind gravestones,
women were screaming, men were shouting,
       the gunman was smiling.

He then began firing in a steady line across the crowd,
       from his left,
causing a sweeping domino-effect, like a Mexican wave,
as the mourners ducked behind the headstones.
       I waited,
then ducked as he levelled his pistol to me.

I held my face to the inscription on someone's headstone,
their life surmised into two monumental dates,
while the wave fell away to my left, the gunshots tracing
      their fatal arc after the falling crest.

Before I stood up, I stole a glance over the headstone.
The gunman had turned and was running towards
the motorway where a white RUC van was parked
on the grass verge. A large group of people chased
after him—unarmed hares
      bolting blindly after the greyhound.

The gunman stopped to turn and fire—the people chasing him
      dodged their heads like boxers weaving fists.
The RUC van drove off. With no bullets left, no grenades,
exhausted, the gunman ran onto the deserted motorway
      chased by three angry men.

At the graveside, film crews scrambled out from behind
their protective tombstones, cameras rolling, frantic for interviews.

A tall, blonde presenter for the BBC with her microphone
      held out like a pistol
turned to me and demanded: *what did you see*? As I turned away,
I told her what anyone from there, in those days, would say:
      'I saw nothing.'

Paul McMahon

Katharine
Oliver Arnoldi

She had been hanging there for a day when they found her. She was young and lithe from what they could tell, with pure pale skin that had started to turn grey. They all agreed that she had once radiated a real beauty. A beauty that had, perhaps, shone brightly in the empty town they now walked through.

It was dark when they found her, her silhouette dangling lightly beneath the lamppost where she was tied. The soft orange glow that the lamp emitted fell directly onto the crown of her head, as if she was on show. Like an angel coming down to earth, or maybe going up to heaven, some of them said. They couldn't decide which but they agreed she was like Katharine Hepburn in *The Philadelphia Story*—beautiful and unattainable.

Hoisted fourteen feet off the ground, she was, even by the capacities of the tallest men, out of reach. No one could tell how she'd got there. Maybe she really was an angel. She had tousled black hair that shimmered in the lamplight and cascaded over a white linen dress. Her head hung low, but if you looked carefully, you could see the remains of thick black make-up that flicked away from the outer corners of her eyes: a modern Cleopatra. She could have been a picture in a gallery, they said.

But her bare feet—dirtied by the mud, the same mud the men trampled through day after day—brought the muse away from the canvas and back down to earth. This detail disturbed the men, but, like lots of other details in their lives, it remained unspoken. Yet it was there, like a tapeworm that eats away at you until its presence is as clear as day.

It was the feet that led them to look to the rest of her body for other disturbances. Hung around her neck was a wooden sign, inscribed with delicate white lettering, which read: '*Ich wollte meine Kinder nicht kämpfen lassen.*'

None of them understood what it meant, and none of them wanted to, for panic of making Katharine less beautiful than she was. So after much discussion they decided it said: 'Will my kind night campers listen.' They couldn't decide what '*Ich*' was—though they'd heard it spoken, they'd never seen it written down—but it was the shortest word in the sentence so it didn't matter. What mattered was Katharine.

The men had time to get to know her for they were waiting rather than fighting. It was the start of May 1945. Berlin was encircled, Hitler dead. The Allies were happy and expectant. So too, it seemed, were the men. But the war had been long and hard.

Katharine offered something different to each of them, at different moments of the day. For Jackson, she was an audience as he oiled the parts of his Jungle Carbine in the midday sun. He would tell her jokes, which he enjoyed, as Katharine always found them funny. Found them funnier than any girl he'd ever met. And she would never stop him telling jokes either, which was even better. She would not order him to straighten up or shout and leave the room. He could stop talking when he wanted to, when his gun was clean.

For Blake, Katharine reinvigorated a more base pleasure. The well-thumbed pin-ups that he carried in his pack had lately provoked a listlessness within him. He was numb to his stained spread of Rita Hayworth, the same spread that every soldier used to escape into the night. The same war, the same guns, the same cigarettes, food and clothes. The same girl. He wanted more than the negligée and the silk sheets, the push-up bra and the fuck-me-eyes. He craved something pure. He wanted to know someone.

Katharine was pure for others too. She was the purest thing McConville had experienced since killing his first animal on the farm. It was a piglet, he remembered, a small thing that squealed that he was told needed to go. He remembered the colours: the pink on top of the white snow that had settled across the field that morning. How cold his hands were against the knife. How red the blood was that ran into the white. He remembered the piercing scream that followed a few hours later from inside the barn, of his mother trying to reach his sister. That dangling rope. He remembered this now with such clarity. A divine icon—a resurrection, maybe—had finally appeared. So it was Katharine that McConville would kneel before when saying his Hail Marys in the morning.

These times of quiet companionship were important for the men. They became the night campers and the empty town became known as Katharine. Katharine, herself, quickly became one of their group. The nights were long so they sat around a bonfire for hours on end, constructed not for warmth but so they could be close to her. McConville liked the way the flames lit Katharine up. The men would bicker over who would tell her the best anecdotes of war. The funny ones, the masculine ones, the stupid ones—never the scary ones.

Telling stories about home often eluded the men, but Katharine opened them up.

'I was a teacher, a real good one. I've always liked children. And the school was nice, too. I remember...'

But when they tried, they only got so far. Details, like names and faces, were not always remembered. Some of the men couldn't quite get their mouths around their memories. Jackson, the teacher, stopped and felt his head like he'd lost something. Then he stared into the fire.

When it got too late to sit around her, they let the fire burn out and walked to a small beer hall, abandoned like the rest of the town. They had to light candles as there was no electricity. It was a tired room, veiled in dust, but some details of its former life still remained. A newspaper lay folded on a table, and a smart hat hung on a stand by the door. The bar was a long wooden one, worn down by the arms of phantom revelers. The beer—the sweet smell of which stained the air—was stale. But they drank it anyway until they felt heavy and foolish.

It was then that they changed, like werewolves in thrall to moonlight. The tables and chairs were cleared to make way for a hazy square outlined by hazy men. Their noises became angry. They removed their shirts and then they fought, one on one, until life got beaten back into them.

'Go on you fuck, give him one.'

'What are you waiting for, beat the cunt!'

'Fuck him up! Fuck him up!'

You couldn't tell who was saying what. More beer flowed and so did blood. Sometimes teeth rolled, catching the dust. When someone was badly beaten, a man or two cast an eye upwards and some guilt escaped towards the ceiling. But Katharine was not there, so they quickly recast their eyes to the fight, hoping no one had spotted their flickering gaze.

Without Katharine's presence, the night did not end until it ended. Only the light that streamed through the window at five revealed the traces of blood and bone and ennui that told the men it was time to sleep.

These rituals of day and night became their routine; it was therapeutic, they told themselves.

McConville never slept, really. He hadn't really slept for the entire war. So he liked spending time with Katharine in the early morning, when the rest of the men were sleeping and the sun didn't beat down on his pale skin. It was because of this that he noticed it first. Something had changed since the men said goodbye to her the night before. From afar, it looked like Katharine had done something to her hair, maybe, or had removed her eye make-up, but as McConville got closer, he realised the difference. Her right eye was gone. His gait slowed and the world zeroed in on the hole. A solar eclipse, big in the sky. He didn't want to go closer but he did, too. As he did, his stare lost focus and his soul unravelled.

She had developed a belly that made her dress bulge, and her skin glistened with welts. From her left eye, a protracted tear of yellow-red fluid trailed her cheek. Flies buzzed. She had acquired the smell of a wet foot left too long in a boot. The smell was all over her and the heat had made it into something intoxicating, a sick sour perfume. She hung heavily, wanting to fall.

As McConville adjusted to the view, his knees quivered. Not with fear—that would come later—but anger. He lit a cigarette, his last one, and blew the smoke directly at Katharine in an attempt to deny her. He blew and blew until only the end remained, but as the smoke lifted, it distilled the new vision. She was an ungodly bitch.

It was a betrayal, the men agreed once they woke. She was fucking ugly now. What did she think she was doing? She couldn't walk away from them. She couldn't change like this. What was Blake meant to do? Who was Jackson going to tell his jokes to?

Speaking about Katharine pulled the men close together again, not as brothers in arms but as a pack of wolves. They'd escaped through the bar door and into the light.

That afternoon they acted in utter unison. They would ignore her for a while, to teach her a lesson. So they shouted songs until hoarse and sprayed bullets into grey streets. They tore up their uniforms. They painted their faces and wrestled in the mud. They jeered and grimaced all as one, away from Katharine, but they had lost any sense of reality. Speech was too conscious, laughter too premature, and they wrestled like they couldn't let go. They were too in need of the human touch. The tapeworm began to exact its presence. You'd look into their eyes and they simply weren't there.

As dusk settled, so did the urge for the routine of the recent past. They wouldn't admit it but they missed her, desperately needed her, in the way that McConville's knees still quivered and Blake's pupils bulged out of his eyes and Jackson's teeth chattered in the heat. They were a soldier who had held his breath too long, veins popping. So they turned and ran to her. They were coming home. They gathered around the ashes of last night's bonfire and sang another song. This time with her included, but they didn't notice whether she joined in as they were singing so loudly. They lit a fire and piled on more wood. They didn't notice the missing eye or the welts or the sick sour smell. None of that mattered anymore—they were on the far side of themselves.

As the wood began to burn, they settled into conversations. They were talking and talking but words—or at least the right ones—weren't coming out. It was all gobbledygook, like the white lettering on the sign that hung round Katharine's neck. They realised that she wasn't there for them like she used to be. She wasn't listening at all. They got on their feet and they screamed at her but she wasn't pulling them back into the world. She had set sail with it across a void that was ever increasing.

'Maybe we need to be closer?' a voice called out.

The men shouted in approval. Without waiting, Jackson raced through the fire and sprang onto the post. He climbed like a monkey, his knife gripped between his teeth. After every metre he turned around to them with a look that cut through the flames and gave the men a wild hope. Once he reached the top, he took the knife into his hand and banged the hollow pipe. They were closer now. They shrieked as he began to cut the rope. He shredded it and as he did so Katharine began to sway, as if he was reanimating her. The men roared when Jackson finished. Katharine fell hard into the mud and they rushed to her like bees protecting their queen. They held onto her as tight as they could. Their nails dug deep. They still didn't notice the missing eye or the welts or the sick sour smell. They just needed to be held but she wasn't holding them back. Her body started to judder: an arm was punching her. Then all the men felt themselves punching her, uncontrollably, in unison. And then they heard a shot.

Blake had pulled the trigger. He pulled again, and again, and once more for luck. In that moment, they couldn't sense her anymore; she had gone beyond the horizon. She was dead and so were they. Dead beyond doubt, and they had enjoyed killing her. It felt so good.

Blake grabbed her arms and Jackson took her legs. No one stopped them. They began swinging her up and down as if playing with a child. The perfect mix of fear and fun, though they didn't need to stop at fun. They could continue. They could really go for it.

They let go of her. Her rotting weight meant she did not fly high like a child can, but collapsed onto the fire like a sack of shit. Silence. Her distended belly popped like a balloon. Jackson sniggered.

As the flames enveloped the body, the fallen world they found themselves in became clearer. Clearer with every shout, with every laugh and stare, until they realised that they too had fallen.

There was no affirmation of what they had done, no post-match team talk. Just stillness, and then, like spectres in the moonlight, the men melted away until only McConville remained.

He laughed, a quiet chuckle. He wasn't sure what to do. So he began speaking, anything that would come out. He blabbered a bit but then found his stride: 'Hail... Hail Mary full of grace The Lord is with thee Blessed art thou among women and blessed is the fruit of thy womb Jesus Holy Mary Mother of God pray for us sinners now and at the hour of our death Amen.' He said it again and again, faster each time. Then slowed down. Then stopped altogether.

As he kissed the crucifix that dangled from his neck, he turned away from the disintegrating figure into the blackness. He howled into it. For the emptiness, the loss of beauty. He thumped his head and stomped hard on the mud.

He felt nothing, nothing but the irregular beating of his heart, a gift from his father.

After a while, he turned back to the fire for light, almost forgetting that he had company. But there she was, it was undeniable. She was so radiant without the men, so McConville sat back down and watched her. He watched her burn, crackle, explode for their sins, like a Roman candle into the night.

RE:*fresh* | *House of Leaves* by Mark Z. Danielewski
Philip St John

I remember my first look inside *House of Leaves*, in Waterstones, back in 2000. Some crazed designer, or vandal, seemed to have rearranged the interior of The Novel. Dense text in a variety of fonts, floods of footnotes, words spiralling, words turning upside down, words thinning to one or two per page, pages with diagrams, pages with squares of foreign text inserted into narrative, an *index*.

Ambitious fiction appeals to me, but I also enjoy a story. Not very hopeful of finding one, but still under the spell of the intriguing cover, a sepia-toned image of a door opening into darkness, I flipped through a few pages and started to read and minutes later found myself at the till buying the tome that occupies one of the Crucial Shelves at my back as I write.

In the passage I happened upon, Will and Karen Navidson and their children are moving into an old house on Ash Tree Lane in rural Virginia. Will, a photojournalist, is supposedly intent on saving their marriage. Obsessed by his often dangerous work in distant troubled spots, he has neglected Karen, and fearful of losing her, all he wants now—he says—is 'a cosy little outpost for me and my family. A place to drink lemonade on the porch and watch the sun set.' Predictably, given the genre, the house has other ideas, though they're not remotely the sort you'd expect.

Will, it turns out, hasn't really kicked his compulsive work habit. He has brought his work home. Funded by grants, he is filming the family's experience of moving into the house, and his camera captures the first, quiet intrusion of strangeness into their new lives. In a wall of the living room is a door. He and Karen haven't noticed it until now and are giddy at the discovery. Then Will opens it. Inside is a hallway ten feet long, cold and dark. Yet when he goes into the garden to film the wall's exterior, there is no sign of any hallway, 'no ten foot protuberance, just rose-bushes, a muddy dart gun, and the translucent summer air.'

Other doorways into paradoxical space appear. Will discovers that the house is a quarter inch bigger inside than outside, and that the hallways behind the multiplying doors are growing, spectacularly. Weighed down with provisions, he and some companions make days-long expeditions through labyrinthine corridors. An enormous staircase takes many hours to descend. From somewhere out in the dark, cold, shape-shifting network of passages, comes an ominous growling.

On re-reading, these passages proved as heart-stopping as they had back in the millennium when I disappeared for a week into *House of Leaves*. I wondered what it was that made them so scary.

Like any great horror story, this one takes us right up to the Inhuman and seems to abandon us there, powerless and uncomprehending as a small child. Danielewski has that gift. He bypasses our critical faculties and goes straight to work on our spines. This doesn't seem to me a result of craft. The prose is strong, and he understands his world's logic and illogic: he has lived there imaginatively. But as we all know from reading inert horror, sometimes even the best writers do not have that primal power; they can't make us start, or see threat in a familiar door.

And then, the newness of Danielewski's tunnel-scapes really makes us attend. We have encountered Contingent Worlds in other books, but this is different; it's not Narnia for grown-ups. The laws, if there are any, are difficult to grasp. Does this world have malign intent? Or is it indifferent: are the torments that Will and his companions suffer simple bad luck? Because we are unsure, because we are constantly forced to process events, while also keeping half-an-eye on what might come at us next, we are really *in* the story, as open to its wonders and horrors as the early readers of *Frankenstein* or *Strange Case of Dr Jekyll and Mr Hyde* must have been.

It also struck me as important that this was not a weird new world far, far away. The labyrinth is in or of the Navidsons' home. While Will ventures through the tunnels, encountering deprivations, violence and terror, the rest of the Navidsons continue, for a time, to live in the sunlit house on Ash Tree Lane. The children are distressed. Karen is seriously disaffected. So the book feels as rooted in realism as Austen or McGahern.

Yet, for me, none of that really explained what made the extraordinary occurrences on Ash Tree Lane feel more *real* than much of the so-called realism I have read in the last decade and a half. I began to wonder if the answer lay with tattooist Johnny Truant.

Much of the novel is about Truant. I'd forgotten how much. Truant hadn't made that great an impression on me. Of course, any narrative running parallel to the Ash Tree Lane one is bound to be eclipsed by it. Maybe that's an unfortunate truth about story-telling. In a multi-stranded tale, there is a risk that one strand will burn more brightly in the memory.

Truant had a very difficult childhood and is now a very troubled young man. He drinks and drugs a lot and sleeps with a lot of women. But it is only when he starts reading about the house on Ash Tree Lane that he begins to come apart. He can't sleep, concentrate, control his thoughts. He loses his job, doesn't leave his flat for days, neglects his appearance. If the story of the house shakes us, it's destroying Truant. But then he is not only reading it, like each of us, alone: in the universe of this novel, he is the *sole* person reading it. Johnny hasn't come across the Navidsons and their portal-afflicted home in a book on a table in Waterstones. He found it inside an old trunk belonging to the late, blind Mr Zampano, who wrote the story on countless scraps of paper ('old napkins, the tattered edges of an envelope, once even… the back of a postage stamp'). Fascinated, haunted, Johnny has collated the writings, annotated them, and written about the terrible effect they've had on him, then passed his and Zampano's words along to unnamed editors who have added further notes and commentary.

In stories, being the possessor of esoteric knowledge can be an insupportable burden. Faust. Macbeth. The antihero isolated by his secret truth. That's one of the reasons Johnny disintegrates, but not the main one. With sardonic authority and convincing detail, Zampano relates the story of the Navidsons as if their ordeal, and the film depicting it, *The Navidson Record*, not only exist but are a focus of cultural controversy. He cites academic publications that squabble over whether the *The Navidson Record* is a brilliantly realised fake documentary, or true to facts. He writes essays on the roles played in the story by echoes, architecture, the *unheimlich*, and labyrinths. He quotes articles that explore the psychology of Will and Karen, appraise Will's cinematic genius, and upbraid Karen for having an affair. The footnotes, citations and allusions are as vast and, yes, labyrinthine, as the corridors explored by Will, yet Johnny Truant can find in 'his' world no trace of this exhaustively analysed film: *The Navidson Record* and all the babble about it do not seem to exist. Could Zampano really have invented this complex and vivid story, and supplied the vast commentary on it? Why would he? Or is Johnny Truant going mad? Is the book making him mad? Has it, even, *picked on* this vulnerable young man?

Though at times he speaks from the pages of *House of Leaves* at such a high pitch of feeling that I wanted him to back off, I couldn't help rooting for Johnny. He's one of us, a reader. His response to the horror is ours intensified. But he also— to use a word that tolls throughout the book—echoes us in a more unsettling way. Reading about how Zampano's apparently invented narrative somehow passes into Johnny's world, traumatising him, I had the creepy sensation *House Of Leaves* was doing something analogous to me. Johnny is crucial to that effect. On its own, the Ash Tree Lane story is merely a fantastic yarn: when it dawns on us that it, and Johnny, are caught at the centre of a vast postmodern web of opinion, rumour, theory, critiques, commentary, crazily detailed citations, notes, diagrams and ephemera, suddenly Johnny and Ash Tree Lane *are* our world. Wordsworth and Heidegger rub up against quotes from a morning TV show. Truant's drug-fuelled theories collide with the sober intrusions of the unnamed editors. Sense bumps into nonsense, trivia into madness, pithiness into exhaustive lists. Sometimes following the thread of the main story in this blare of distractions becomes as maddeningly difficult as trying to read in a public place full of flashing screens and people shouting into phones. But that's how the novel captures like no other I can think of our contemporary information overload. Ash Tree Lane belongs to us, now, in a way that old castles, creepy moorlands and Mordor no longer do. We are living inside the book.

Is this what Danielewski's novel is about then: data-deluge? At times I thought so, but like the shape-shifting tunnels on Ash Tree Lane, *House of Leaves* keeps updating under the reader's gaze. Again and again, I had to revise my understanding of what the book was up to. It's about marriage. No, a macho male's need to prove himself. No, it shows how a family, in the absence of threat, will create its own danger. Sorry—it's about America: the haunting of the Ash Tree area precedes the first settlers, after all. No, it's a satire on the crazed attention we focus on celebrated people, places and events. No, no, clearly it's a prescient evocation of the consequences of the Net: we can close the doors, put on the alarm, but there are still portals; things enter, we exit, lose ourselves... As I came to its last pages, I began to realise that I still hadn't quite 'got' *House of Leaves* and that, like the other great works of fiction on my Crucial Shelves, it would eventually lure me back for another exploration of its haunting maze of resonances.

today has its genesis in the game-changing study by R'lyeh University that began in 2028. We pioneered the development of microspheres and their application in targeted drug delivery: extending life spans, eradicating disease, completely upending contemporary models for best practice in medicine.

So should we have just stopped there, rested on our laurels? No, we had to follow what was in our hearts. We kept our eyes firmly focused on tomorrow. It wasn't sufficient that we could stop disease in its tracks; we needed to be able to repair and regenerate. So we looked next to the true building blocks of human life – stem cells. Early breakthrough developments that allowed us to convince adult stem cells to revert to an embryotic stage were critical - in this early stage, the stem cells have the potential to become any type of cell in the body. This gave us the capacity to engineer and intervene to restore or establish normal function.

So, ok, tell me, should we have just stopped there, rested on our laurels? No, we had to follow what was in our hearts. And we went outside the box, way outside the box.

Why weren't we content with creating health and extended longevity for people? Because the notion itself limited our progress – sure, we could improve the length and quality of people's lives but this was always constrained by the idea that they were people, and therefore, by necessity, mortal. Not only mortal, but humans can't fly, can't live underwater, can't make themselves invisible, can't outrun a car. So why should we limit ourselves to within these parameters?

It was time to look outside those parameters, to the natural world, to the animal kingdom and beyond. To the fish, to the frogs. To bodies that not only can be regenerated, but which are inherently designed to regenerate themselves.

It has been twenty years since the first pioneering experiments that created **Xenopthor**, the prototype of the **Xenophon** species, in 2040. It has been two short years since the first successful births of laboratory-engineered since conception para-humans, born in 2058. We don't know what their future holds, but they surely won't be alone – they will be joined by brothers and sisters later this year.

Look closely at this, the pinnacle of our creation, the long-anticipated, custom-designed, zebrafish-hybrid heart, tailored for the next gen of para-human. Strong, self-repairing, resilient, enduring.

We don't know if this gen, or the next, will live forever. We do know that our concepts of a human lifespan, even at its most extended, hold no relevance to them. The diseases mankind has fought to cure, eradicate, prevent are, again, entirely irrelevant to

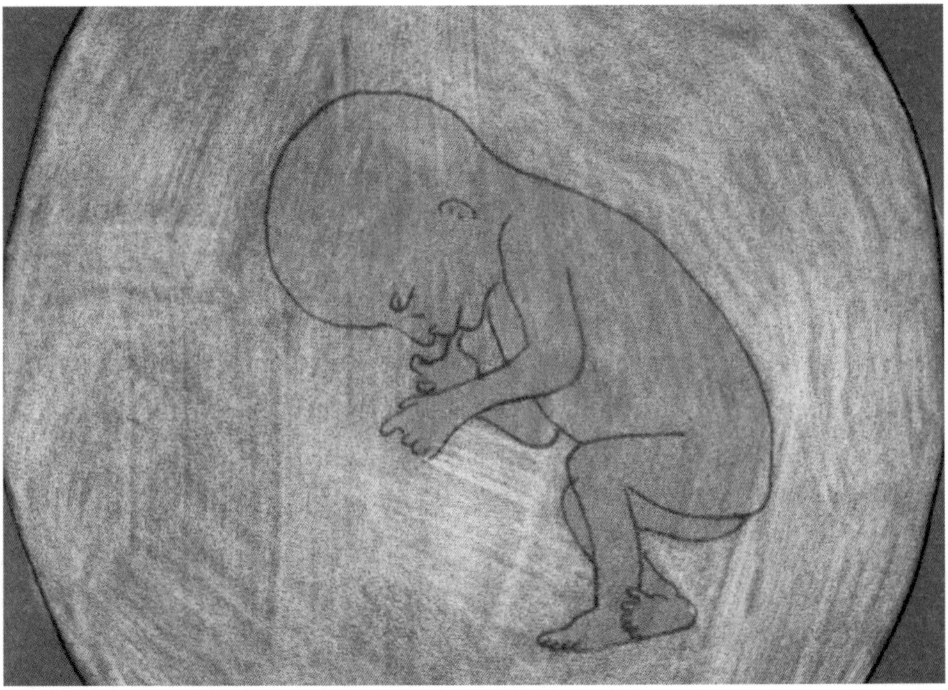

The Shroud

What the boy draws happens.
He sketched an orange this afternoon.
Nice still life, I thought
until the winter sky
spawned a vermilion moon.

On his bedside locker this morning,
a jungle scene. When I saw
the stems that the geraniums
sprouted over lunch,
the glass in my hand smashed on the tiles.

Later, a back leg snapped off my chair
and I scalded myself with tea. A fist
of paper in his wastebasket smoothed to reveal
three tall S's rising from a mug
on a three-legged seat.

I confiscated every sketch pad and page,
pencil, crayon and pen in the house.
Not an hour after, I found him on his knees,
working a nugget of coal across my best blouse.
Seeing me, he dropped it onto—a face?

You can't imagine how tightly I grip
the banister whenever I descend stairs,
my anxiety at the line of light
under his bedroom door.
Truly, I dread the holidays.

Evan Costigan

Amelia Magdalene
Heather Parry

It was a blessing when my blood came. At school they said it would be spots and strings but to my surprise it was a steady stream, dark red, pouring out from the corners of my eyes and puddling on the tops of my battered brogues. I held back a retch and when the urge to faint passed, I shouted for Daddy, excited, from the top of the stairs. Squinting into the light from the landing, he said: *God bless us, Joyce, it's a miracle.* My mother, hunched over like she'd been screwed up and thrown away, strained to look up at me and screamed. As she fled back to her overcooked potatoes, Daddy took the crusty hanky from his back pocket and wiped the blood across my nose and cheeks, making more of a mess than there was before. He shoved the hanky into my hand. Grinning, grateful, I took in the acrid smell and pocketed the soaked cotton. Daddy strode into the kitchen, and I heard his giddy voice rise:

Hospital? She needs an agent, not a hospital.

There were to be no doctors. Daddy's word was always final, not because he was the stronger of the two, but the weaker. My mother's twisted spine—she'd been that way all my life—brought disability benefit into the house and gave her a quiet dignity; Daddy's consistent inability to find work, despite trying, only made him more pathetic. Yet he ruled with a ceaseless sense of enthusiasm that nobody could bear to wrench from him. My first thought when I looked into the mirror and saw two trickles of scarlet running from my eyes had been: *Daddy is going to love this.*

That night, he watched me over dinner, wads of old tea towels taped to my cheeks so the blood wouldn't drip onto my eggs. My mother fretted over the creeping red cracks in the whites of my eyes but Daddy just stared. Sometimes he smiled, and sometimes I smiled back.

The office of Oswald Merman was white and gold, a dressing room for potential starlets; a mock Versailles. All platinum blonde and crisp white cotton with a shock of electric blue beneath his lapels, Merman tentatively reached over to his phone, side-eying me like I was a glass of red wine waiting to tip. Daddy patted my arm again—to relax himself rather than me, I knew—and nodded to no one in particular, his greying head bobbing like a plastic dog on the back shelf of someone's car. A silicone baby bib, complete with a crumb-catcher that had to be emptied every couple of hours, hung from my ears and fit tightly around my chin.

Cynthia, could you get the Vatican on the phone? I've no idea, you'll have to look in the yellow book.

They were saying things like *percentage cut* and *security detail* and *power of attorney*. I squinted at the portrait over Merman's shoulder to see if it was of a man or a woman. Everything was opaque and lacked edges. My hands twitched, itching to wipe and scratch at my sore sockets, but I knew Daddy needed me not to. I buried my fingers beneath my bottom. My eyelids worked overtime but still couldn't wipe my vision clean so I closed them, letting the sound of Merman's words distract me.

Oh. It seems to have… Mr. Parsons?

The raw liver dissolved on my tongue and Daddy nodded encouragingly, pretending that neither of us could hear my mother vomiting into the kitchen bin. Liver for lunch, kidneys for dinner, black pudding for breakfast; it was my new regime, intended to bring back the blood tears that had dried up, seemingly of their own accord, right before Daddy signed my name on Merman's dotted line. Daddy thought it was a lack of iron, or plasma, or something or other that he'd read in the mouldy medical books now stacked in the bathroom. Mother told him it was just one of those things. Each morning he checked my sheets for stains, running into my room when he heard me close the bathroom door, then scuttling dejectedly down the stairs to my mother as he heard me flush.

Three weeks later, Daddy had cultivated quite the relationship with the local butcher, who loved his spike in profits, but my eyes were still dry, the skin around them recovering slowly. The details of my world were starting to come back into focus and it seemed like everything was returning to normal, the episode a single occurrence destined to be remembered in parenthesis. Daddy's panicked positivity, however, could not be quelled. On the Monday, he announced that my diet was doubling. On the Thursday, I woke with a thin bolt of pain running across my torso and I spent the day in bed, tended to by my limping mother, while Daddy fed me liver smoothies and kidney soup and examined the veins in my arms when he thought I wasn't looking.

On the Saturday, the red tears came once again, this time with errant stringy lumps that I had to pull past my tear ducts and away from the path to my mouth.

It's her monthlies, said my mother. *By God, it's her curse.*

Daddy got me a bruised Bible from the local charity shop and an off-white dress that touched the tops of my toes. To watch him working, creating, brought a warmth to my face; he'd always been an inventor on the side. When I was two, it was a stuffed toy with a heat-pad stomach and a clock inside that burned my thigh and gave me tinnitus. Just after I'd started school, it was an electrical washing-up device with robot arms that fell into the sink and caused a kitchen fire. When I was five years old my mother lost her eyebrows in a complicated incident involving a mechanical set-up that pulled the sheets back every morning. But he needed the hope, the belief that someday his name would be attached to something great, so we kept our mouths shut when he sunk more of our savings into his projects and negated the house insurance time and time again.

But Daddy, I told him, *I can't see the words*, as he showed me the passages that he'd underlined during a sleepless night of planning. He read the verses to me as he fed me orange juice and Pop Tarts, a sweet treat after so much offal, and I got so good at repeating them back between sugary mouthfuls that neither of us heard my mother's frantic yelps until she'd been calling for thirty minutes. With no one to help her reach the wall-mounted rail that allowed her to get out of bed, she'd stretched too far and fallen, her cheek grazing the unvarnished wood of my parents' bedroom floor. We hauled her up to her feet but her spine, robbed of its morning exercise, had locked itself into an angry question mark, an exaggeration of her normal condition. I wrapped my legs around her and massaged the spaces between her vertebrae. Daddy said that once we'd made it to our meeting, she could take the car and drive herself to the hospital.

Merman had told the others waiting in his antechamber—six-fingered boys, morbidly obese teens, women with well-groomed facial hair—that he wasn't taking any more appointments. They trudged out mournfully as the three of us followed Cynthia, who seated us briskly, then dispensed sugary black coffees that we had not ordered and did not want. Merman asked Daddy question after question. My mother, unwilling to leave me, held my hand, her eyes closed, her palm spasming in pain from time to time. Cynthia, disgusted with the job now taking her away from diarising and coffeemaking, swabbed the sore flesh under my eyes and apologised curtly before sealing the cotton in a test tube and noting the date on the label. I stood up and she patted me down, running her hands between my aching breasts and up my back to feel for plastic lines or other trickery. She patted my shoulder and nodded. Seeing that we were done, my mother uncurled herself and slipped her arm around my waist, unburdening some of her weight, as she led me out to our Volvo.

Apologies, Angelo, I heard Merman say to Daddy as my mother and I left the office. *I've got to be sure; too many court cases these days, you know. Now, let's talk scheduling.*

Before I could say anything to the hospital receptionist, my mother reached across the desk, grabbed both of the woman's grey hands and said, *Please, you've got to help my daughter*. There were gasps as the strangers on the plastic chairs forgot their personal maladies and turned around to look at me. The receptionist, shaken, led us straight through to an examination room. My mother talked over me every time I tried to insist that we were there for her, the agony in her back. One doctor came, then two, then other fuzzy figures in white coats and blue scrubs filled up the less distinct corners of the room. My virginity was taken on crunchy hospital paper by a smooth piece of cold metal, with a mass of medical staff staring between my spread legs and my mother holding my hand. The hysteroscope projected a moving image onto the plasma screen by my head, but all I could see was a mass of flesh that looked like it was crawling. I stared at the ceiling until the cold thing slid out of me, unsure of whether to feel ashamed, embarrassed or proud.

Well, it's just the strangest thing. She's wired perfectly, Mrs. Parsons. The lining's all there. It's just not coming out where it's meant to.

My mother asked if I'd have babies still, and though the doctor said that he couldn't see why not, someone right by my head huffed and said, *I think someone's got other plans for that girl.*

They prescribed me drops for my stinging eyeballs and arranged an appointment with specialists from the mainland. A week later when the letter dropped on the mat, Daddy barely glanced at the headed paper before he tore it into pieces with a pained grin on his face, saying through gritted teeth, *But Darling, you're going to be famous!*

After that, there was no time for school. With just twenty-one days until my inaugural performance and only seven potential show days per month, it was rehearsals from the moment my tears dried to the moment they came again. I started to think of time only in cycles of twenty-eight days. Merman closed his offices and came over every morning, calling me things like *Our Starlet* and touching the ends of my hair. My mother stayed in the kitchen while I recited verses in the glow of a makeshift spotlight, but she made me a cucumber eye-mask to soothe my aching sockets and defied Daddy's carnivorous diet plan by feeding me cold carrot juice every night. Daddy and Merman broke the lock on my diary to check the dates of my cycle and draw up a schedule, and on day twenty-seven of that month I was christened and reborn; the name in neon lights was Amelia Magdalene.

All press is good press, beamed Merman as he paced excitedly around me, brandishing a national newspaper that, they told me, had my school photo on the front. He and Daddy were too busy planning PR responses to tell me what it said, but my mother had taken a break from our rehearsals to read the whole thing out loud. A reporter had paid our next-door neighbour a grand to steal the liver-smeared blender from our kitchen, and the resulting article was a blizzard of insult and conjecture, calling me a fraud and Daddy a liar.

We'll put up the ticket prices by half, said Merman. *You're a bona fide star now, girl.* He grabbed me by the shoulder, then grimaced as he wiped my mess from his forearm. I could still catch the shimmer of him in the dim light of the dressing room as he swam around in the near dark, a siren for those seeking salvation. He and Daddy disappeared into a shadowy corner and said things like *defamation* and *libel* and *great publicity*. I closed my sore eyelids and let the words of the Lord, recited by my mother, drown out the cold phrases of business.

It turned out that Merman was right. We moved to larger venues, auditoriums that had no ceilings and theatres so old that they had no lifts. My mother had to drag herself up spiral staircases behind my growing entourage. After I'd been on the evening news, Daddy bought me designer glasses with the name of a footballer's wife on the side. They shielded me from the lightning bolts of cameras and, as Daddy put it, *protected our best assets*. With every show, details dropped away and my depth perception suffered. My mother taught me to see by feel, running my hands over the dressing tables and plush sofas in every new city, keeping my fingers away from my face lest I ruin the perfect streams.

We touched down in France on a Tuesday. The flights had been booked so that I'd already be bleeding, ready for the press on the runway, but we arrived late after a delay of six panicked hours when the miracle had declined to begin at its scheduled time. I could see too much; the light was more than I had glimpsed in months. I clutched my boarding pass and willed the tears to come. Daddy prayed and Merman barked at anonymous assistants, ordering them to bring ten feet of plastic tubing and an IV bag. Airport authorities fussed and snarled in the doorway of the first-class lounge and were shooed away by the lurching lump of my mother. I lay down with my head in Daddy's lap and drowsed off while Merman measured my torso. When I finally blinked awake, the world was shadowed once more and a cheer went up in the room. Three hours later we landed in Lourdes, the heat of the air making my tears drip faster as my mother described the thousands waiting on the airstrip. Their weeping hymns brought up the goosebumps on my arms and made me hold Daddy's hand a little tighter.

There were three performances a day, each one attended by two hundred more than could really fit into the Church of Our Lady, or so I was told, and though the verses had been burned into memory by my mother's ceaseless repetition, I found that my role was much smaller than I'd imagined. I stood in my darkness, arms slightly turned away from my body, and I let them all watch while my uterus lining ran down my face in thick furrows and the priest's words echoed around me. I spoke only when prompted, a few lines about forgiveness, and held my palms out to be kissed by the mouths of a thousand faceless strangers when the priest pushed me to my knees at the edge of the stage.

We upped the schedule to six shows a day, my eyes settling into a quiet but constant pain that coated the inside of my skull. I touched a fingertip to my cheek and licked the wetness there to know if the show could still go on; it stopped tasting metallic on day eight, though Daddy said we'd been blessed with one more day than normal because we were doing God's will.

That final day in Lourdes was one long performance. The priest took my hands and placed them on the broken bodies of those with unworking limbs and skin ravaged by disease, their pustules and bedsores oozing beneath my fingertips while they told me of week-long journeys from Israel, Australia, Ireland and beyond. *Twelve thousand*, someone said, as silhouettes came and went before my outstretched palms. Daddy brought me ice-cream and juice, the sweetness punctuating seven sour days of steak tartare and the body of Christ, and as I felt the warmth of the sun burn through stained-glass windows I prayed to keep feeling the glow of Daddy's happiness.

Seven weeks later I realised that we weren't going home.

I never saw Italy. The tyres touched the tarmac on day twenty-eight of my ninth cycle, to give us time to settle in before the main event and recover from the righteous insanity of Guatemala. Daddy gripped me, quivering with joy at having finally become somebody, the father of a miracle child, as he described the hordes of believers raising their hands from their eyelids to the skies in worship, thanking the Lord himself for his blessing. Not a word reached my ears, though, as I was lifted by thick biceps into a vehicle—an armoured limo, Merman said—and handed a glass of something fizzy that tingled up my nose. My mother pressed my hands against the walls of the hotel, which were patterned with velvet, and she told me that within the grand suite there were rooms enough for each of us, though Daddy slept atop my covers, waking hourly to check with the large men at my doorway. The next morning, I woke on my back with my arms straight out from my shoulders and still not touching the sides of the mattress, adrift in an endless sea of decadence. All the light had gone from the world, though, even the shadows, even the shapes. My eyes were weeping, but it tasted yellow, of pus, and my mother coughed out an embittered cry when I staggered, unseeing, from my haven.

*

There must have been a number of different doctors, all speaking in tongues, none saying a word to me. Merman yelled at translators at the foot of my bed as gloved fingers dabbed and touched and bathed and anointed me. The weathered skin of my mother's hands, the skin of a hard life, rested on my forehead. I listened to the constant low moan that had replaced her voice.

Just make it stop, will you? snapped Merman. *Not antibiotics, we need something that will work right now!*

Arguments broke out and I clutched my mother's thigh, willing myself into sleep so I didn't have to hear. I woke to the rustle of sheets that smelled clinical, the clatter of metal instruments and the aggressive heat of lamps not far from my face. With a little pressure and a nick on my inner arm, they told me to count back from ten, and by four I fell into a woolly unconsciousness. When I came around, there were tight, stinging lines under my eyes, the flesh throbbing. Someone applied a drizzle of liquid that burned right through to my ear. A heavily accented voice spoke just before tablets were put in my mouth and my throat was rubbed to make me swallow as if I were a recalcitrant cat.

The drainage was successful but the infection might still come back. She'll need the medication for at least ten days, but I urge you to cancel the meeting. That girl needs a hospital, not a blessing.

The next morning the metallic taste dripped into my mouth and my tear ducts ached. I pulled gently and removed thick clumps of menstrual blood from just below my eyeballs, my face still puffy and painful, my mind still cloudy and warm. My body and head were covered in a coarse material, the thick cotton cutting around my neck. Sharp fingernails applied thick-scented lotions and powders to my face as Daddy and Merman spoke to the press outside the door, and I giggled a painkiller giggle, tickled by the way the brushes caught on my eyelashes. In the early afternoon, a man called from beyond the door and my mother kissed my forehead, halting as if she was going to say something before scurrying away from my bed. A swarm entered the room, the voices all male, and hands carried me out to a car. I couldn't quite grasp onto anything, couldn't quite shake away the fuzziness in my head, and I wondered if it really was Daddy weeping next to me, kissing my hands and calling me an angel. When the car pulled to a halt, delicate fingers dabbed the clotted blood out of my painted eyes and led me out into the harsh sun.

Our steps echoed off marble walls as we entered the building, the searing heat giving way to astonishing cold. I let myself be taken, hushed voices whispering *Holy Father* and *Your Grace*, and when I was put onto my knees I kissed the warm metal on the fingers in front of my mouth, as I had been told to do.

She'll be a saint, said an accented voice, and I thought, *Daddy must be so proud*.

Radium Mother

Marie Curie's cookery book
is so radioactive, they say,
it must be locked in a lead box:

we should wear protective clothes
(white bodyalls, helmet-mask,
lead gloves) to open it and see

the garlic stains, soup splashes,
crushed and stirred and served
by her glow-in-the-dark hands.

Jane Robinson

The Blind Clairvoyant

Baba Vanga, I never heard of you.
You were kept secret by Yeltsin.
But I'm learning about you now—
blind, clairvoyant, prophesying this,
that, and everything. You had to get
some things right – the big tsunami,
the melting polar ice caps, the election
of an African-American US President –
but I'm impressed by the prophecy that
two metal birds would attack New York.
I would never have seen that coming.
You stayed quiet on the moon landings,
and the goal-genius of Lionel Messi,
but I did like your insouciant claim
that aliens are living here for decades.
I often imagined this must be the case—
I even wondered if I might be one.
But what's all this stuff about Isis,
and a Europe as we know it being kaput,
replaced by a Caliphate, with Rome
at its epicentre, all this in ten short years?
Come off it, Baba Vanga. Admit, from
death, that this was maybe a dumb call,
one of your 20 or 30 per cent misfires.

Matthew Sweeney

Joe the Aquanaut and the Aftermath Blue
Oran Ryan

1. I Kept Meeting Myself in Dreams

Back when Commercial Craft Corp ran flights from Jupiter to the holiday centres off Ganymede and Rigel, I flew obnoxious tourists for their summer vacations. It was unchallenging and predictable, but it afforded me a comfortable life. Then, after the lunar real estate boom and economic crash, the work dried up. Being unemployed brought huge pressures on my marriage. Things cracked up. I came home one day and Susie told me she was leaving. She had been having an affair. Then she told me she was pregnant. Within a month, she left me for a research chemist half my age. She had been sleeping with him for years. I never knew. I had always been a pretty rational guy. But I went crazy. I felt humiliated and checkmated. I wanted blood. So I found him late one night coming out of a bar and I gave him a lesson in humility. I figured he wouldn't know who'd hit him. But he knew it was me. And this guy, my wife's future spouse, the well-endowed research chemist Gordon Theodore Andrew Brock the Second, had connections. Now this I didn't know. He fixed me up good. After that incident, I didn't see the kids for years. I lost whatever scraps of jobs I had. So I had to find work. But I couldn't. So I went down into the darkside. I went Skid Row. And there I was, living with two friends, both drug addicts, in Kessel and sleeping through the day. I got addicted to the Skag. Then, disaster. My buddy from the troopers overdosed on the old Skagmeister right next to me. He died in my arms at five in the morning on a warm June day three years after the Great Economic Relaxation. I had to get out. I couldn't live there. If the cops did a blood scan and found me high, I would lose my licence forever. So I cold turkeyed in gutters and sleep halls. Hell. Money ran out. I lived by theft and graft. I got better.

Healthier. I was always robust. Then I got a job. A year afterward, I got back to being a paid astronaut. I started flying small stops between New London and Addis Ababa XII. I was lucky. I mean, I knew things weren't right. I didn't tell the control psychs about the voices I'd seen up on those Rigel flights years before. You can lose your license if you get the space crazies. And I was still addicted. I'd been using the narcs to take the edge off the visions. Now I had no narcs in my system and I was getting the visions again. That was hard. I had always been a rational type. Cold hard logic and all that Boolean stuff. But then came the visions and the voices. Back again. Maybe it was the cold turkey. Skag lingering in the brain cells. It does that. And the longing to get high. Passing asteroid fields that would spell out the future and longing to get high. Ghostly figures in the cockpit telling me about the end of everything, and my longing to get high.

I spent a stint on a space station off Neptune. I was running supply shifts and one night I had the big vision. A vision of the Deep Blue. Let me unpack this: I had a vision of a guy who looked just like me. I kept seeing him. At lunch. In my bunk. In my room. In the control console room. In the cockpit. I said to myself: who am I? I mean, I keep meeting myself. I keep meeting myself and I dunno who I am. There I am—holding a Deep Blue Something in my hands. A deep glowy glowlight. There I am—a Man. Medium Height. Medium Build. Holding a Glowing Blue Cubelike Something. He smiled at me. Do not be afraid, he said. I am with you always. Go down into the Deep Blue. The bog dark. The big freeze. I said, you gotta be shitting me. Don't be afraid? This is the worst, most terrifying thing ever. I said, I know you don't work on this supply vessel. I know you don't have a permit to be on the late night pilots' cockpit. You are not real. You aren't real because you need to have paperwork to be here. I know that. I am in charge here, I said. Now get yourself the hell off my cockpit. And my ghostly ghost, he who looked like me, said that something terrible was going to happen. From that day I lived with a sense of depression, misery, and the voices of doom. I kept them all a secret. Then the doom really came. My ghostly visitor had been right all along. Apocalypse now. Wow. Death, I thought.

2. The Dying Star

The star Lucem Ex Tenebris exploded two hundred and fifty million million light years away. It blew away many thousand star and planetary systems in the wake of its explosion. It sent meteor showers racing in every direction but ours. Then one headed our way. It was big. Really big.

They saw Meteor Tolstoy coming. Bits of a planet. Only one bit of whatever planet Tolstoy was once a part of was coming our way. The others were flying off on differing vectors. Tolstoy's approach was kept hush hush. But an object that big can't be kept secret for long. Soon everybody knew. They sent out attack ships to blow it up. That didn't work. It was too big. Twice the size of Earth. They sent out other killer ships with new high-grade ordnance and blew away parts of it outside Mars. Other bits, however, kept coming towards our soon-to-be-shipwrecked planet. They blew more of those away. Wave after wave. Some even crashed their nuclear craft against it, kamikaze-style. What was left of Tolstoy was only one twentieth the size of Earth when it hit us. It hit west of Indonesia between the islands of Tarawa, Funafuti, and Port Vila, the aftermath tsunami immediately swallowing Australia. Then it drowned Indonesia. It swallowed the Americas. Much of the sea had been rising for decades. It began to devour Asia. It washed over south from St. Petersburg to Yaroslavl, its waters sweeping from Nizhny Novgorod to Kazan, from Chelyabinsk to Omsk, and from Krasnoyarsk to the Sea of Okhotsk. Everything was submerged. As the waters rose, the sun became obsolete. Earth had been punched out of its orbital pathway by Tolstoy. No more photosynthesis. No more air. Plants, animals and insects were facing instant extinction as everything began to get goddamn cold.

Those in the know knew the end was nigh. I knew it because of my visions. The Most Powerful on Earth, those hidden, who control all things unimportant, tried to direct operations from spaceships orbiting the Earth. No one listened. This was because of the plight of the people. Everyone was trying and failing to survive. So the Most Powerful left, abandoning the Earth, despite great misgivings and terrible guilt.

When the Most Powerful were gone, the Richest Families were left. But they all died. The Richest Families died not because they were corrupt and inept and lazy and dependent on the Most Powerful. It was because no one could fight the waves and the consequent freeze. Morality didn't seem a factor in this.

The poets and novelists and the artists found this really ironic. And, always looking for a good drama-filled subject for their art, they worked hard. It kept them in the money and in the news. They wrote and painted and created furiously before they all drowned or died or froze or caught some dreadful infection.

After the Richest Families and the artists were gone, the Think Tanks were left, safe in their subterranean caverns. The Think Tanks sought, and failed, to find an answer to the question of the rising waters and increasing freeze. They transmitted analysis, projections, and measurements worldwide to whatever systems were still operational. Then the most brilliant of them were killed in a freak accident when the power supplying them was cut during a firefight between two military freighters. The firefight had nothing directly to do with the rising waters.

After the Think Tanks were gone, Big Finance started buying up all the available spaceships to take themselves and their top people and their monies off the planet. When Big Finance was gone, having stripped the planet of all assets, there were the Corporations, whose assets were either gone or had drowned in the great cities or were freezing in virtual bank vaults on several planets.

Fast Reaction Teams went out to fix things. Most of them never came back. They were never found and there was a day of mourning for them. Days, by the way, lasted only four hours by then. We were swinging out of orbit of Sol.

Religious leaders proclaimed the Apocalypse. Then they died. The widespread panic got more widespread. There were riots and revolutions and the Governments and the people fought and everyone lost. People saw Government and the Police and the Media and the Family crumbling under the unfolding world catastrophe, so they turned to God and to Knowledge. They thought and prayed and tried solutions. It didn't help. Everyone drowned anyway. Huge ships were crushed beneath waves ten miles high.

I watched the waves. Sometimes we were pulling drowned people up by ropes. The waves were so high you drowned before you reached the craft trying to save you. The waves reached over the highest super-buildings. Horrible sights of unspeakable tragedy greeted survivors everywhere. People had to do desperate, selfish, nasty, survival-of-the-fittest, ruthless things to not die. I worked on. People I met as I flew them to relative safety assumed the cold hollow look of the hopeless and the suffering. Animals and birds and insects and reptiles, creatures who could not breathe in water, if not drowned, then starved to death. The technology that ran things crackled and sputtered out. After that, things got worse.

3. *The Stars Like Ice, The Stars Like Tears...*

The temperature dropped. The Earth had swung out of orbit. The ice came. The Earth, stretching itself out on the invisible ties of gravity, swung out closer to Mars and further from the Sun than it ever had. And, as the North and South poles stretched down like two great hands grasping the planet, drawing the water into themselves in greedy freezing handfuls of ice, everything stopped dead. The sea creatures and animals and insects froze and the people froze and the buildings like refrigerators went hard and cold and the ice came down and the Earth changed from blue to white. And in the frozen water, everything went still and hard, and those who were left built crafts and went south to the equator, for there was a little land left, and they killed each other for soil mainly, for that was what they had always done, and there was so little land left and few people.

In the midst of this, I was hurting badly. I worked on and tried to contact Susie. I was hysterical and sleepless and depressed. I searched refugee camps, floating shelters, previous addresses, everything that wasn't submerged, which was precious little. My sorrow was like those great black waves that had drowned the planet. I felt our separation and divorce had been a terrible mistake, a primitive act based on unresolved issues rather than the deeper love we might have had for each other, a love damaged by life's hardships and failures. I was lonely, filled with regret, but more than anything, filled with denial and a tendency to isealise people, especially Susie. By now, only a few of the great mountains were left. The Alps, the Rockies, the Urals, the Himalayas. People had started living on huge floating ships, all fused together. And I could not find Susie.

Despairing, I went back on the Skag and slept for a month in a remote nuclear ship I found outside Norway. When I woke up, I went back to my search. No answer. My family was now twice lost to me. Then my employers found out about my drug problem. They fired me from my flying job for absenteeism. It was hilariously ironic and futile. I didn't care. I knew that the worst had happened. My Susie was gone. I thought of the effects of discovering her body, beautiful and dead. My heart was dead inside. I decided to abandon the search.

So I got out of there. I took myself down to the bottom of the ocean to explore the underworld. I think I was trying to find somewhere to die. The ship I was in wasn't fit for purpose. But there were endless wrecks, abandoned vessels adrift and unclaimed, great hulking crewless spaceships that lay like dead whales all along the coasts of Napa, London, Murmansk, Southern California. I found a craft listing on its side. Like so many of these vessels, it was a floating coffin. When I came on board, everyone was dead. I dumped the bodies, took it out of sight to a lonely Norwegian fjord, stocked it with food and supplies, and rebooted the droids on board. After a week's work and tooling around, I started the engines. I called it *Lucifer*. I was working against time. There was the freeze and the limited supply of energy cells and the food situation. The engines would burn hydrogen from the water and suddenly, for a bit, bring me anywhere I wanted. Then they would die again. I sat for a long time drinking tea and thinking and reading through the engine specs. It took another week before I finally got them running properly. I looked around. Darkness and death was everywhere. The only thing I had left was my visions. There was nowhere to go but down. I wept and decided I would fix the other computers as I dived. I sealed the craft as the winds and the squall picked up again. Inside myself I felt the chill. It was getting colder.

4. *The Deep*

You have to go down, down into the deep blue, the voice had told me. So down I went. Down the downward spiral. Down past the few threadbare washed-up islands left, with their crumbling half-built cities and few millions, into the desert of the dark. It was a beautiful restful feeling of falling, falling away from humanity's agony, falling away from all the mistakes I had made, the guilt I felt at not being able to save my ex-wife and the kids, two of them mine, the sorrow at a drowned and frozen world above, when down here the ice had not come and would not ever come. Down I went, into the world beneath the world. Down past the dead ships and broken submarines and drowned cities that went on for miles and miles into another world. This dark world was filled with fishes and creatures and mountains and chasms so deep they disappeared into the very core of all that was. In many ways, it was impossible to tell whether I was going up or down, so absolute was the blackness. The only measurement was the gradual increase of pressure, and a clock on the wall of the cockpit that told me, by the ever-increasing numbers, that I was travelling further down than I had ever thought I could. The air scrubbers kept me alive and the packs of protein, carbs and vitamin shakes would last me for months. Since I didn't expect to last as long as months in this absolute blackness, I didn't give long-term survival much thought. I was still trying to cope with all that had happened to the planet.

For as the ship swam in this great plexi-steel part-translucent glass bio-craft that sustained my life, I decided there were a number of things I did not know. I did not know how long I would live. I did not know if anyone else, save the fish and other sea creatures I was seeing now and again, was alive. I did not know what I was going to do in the next few minutes to stay sane. So I made a list of things. I divided up my day between activities. Four to five hours work: cleaning and maintaining the engines and various systems on the ship.

Workout: one hour of stretching, exercises and yoga meditation. Three hours reading and writing and note-taking. One hour washing and cleaning both the ship and myself, and ensuring a basic level of hygiene was maintained so as to avoid infection and contamination of food supplies. Of course this is a very general list. Inevitably things get flexible. One nods off asleep during reading or meditating. Or one reads through a whole book in a 'day'. Or one discovers a huge problem with a system that eats into your whole schedule.

Generally speaking, I divided up the time into a twenty-four hour cycle, and to maintain some kind of circadian rhythm, I switched off the lights for eight of those twenty-four hours. The reactors on the ship kept me warm. I listened to recordings and tapes in order to have some type of voice, a human voice, some voice other than my own, saying something. I listened to most of the world's literature, tried to catch a few of my favourite shows, and most of all, tried to keep busy. I didn't know what else to do. When I thought of my purpose, my goal, as we went down to the bottom of the ocean, *Lucifer* and I, I realised I didn't have one. I didn't even know what I was looking for—just this endless journey into a nothing before and behind me, and a constant worry, despite all my best efforts and organisational skills, that death would come at any second, that this was insane and without purpose, and that perhaps this wasn't really happening, seeing as I had no way of verifying, outside my own senses, that any of it was real.

It is a far better thing I do, I said. It's a far, far better thing. It's better to relax and read novels and not take life too much to heart. Better that than considering the Apocalypse. I feared a return of my depression. That would not be good. Getting terminally depressed down here. It could be terminal. No, I thought. It's a far better thing I do by occasionally repairing things, than constantly worrying over a sudden demise I cannot in the end prevent if structural integrity fails. It was black outside, a kind of infinite black, with only the nudgings and sounds of the deep sea creatures talking to each other and moving past, some bumping against the craft or even against the plexi-glass. But this brought no comfort. It was as though the world was uninhabited. This was ridiculous. We are never alone. And yet we are alone. We have purpose. And yet we have no purpose. We love. And yet we do not really understand the mysteries of love or who or what we love. In the midst of this, I tried to keep calm and carry on. I stuck to my schedule and left unanswerable questions unanswerable. That's my job. Keep calm. Carry on.

5. Lucifer *Finds the Blue*

I realised, possibly too late, that there would never be an end to my ignorance and living in fear. Despite all my efforts, I had been afraid for much of my time underwater. It was probably post-traumatic stress. Depression. Psychosis. Severe anxiety. The usual fare of those who had seen too much. I had seen ships explode, seen everything end, witnessed hundreds die before my eyes, so many dead animals and birds. I was disappointed in myself. I have never experienced the kind of intense selfish fear for my own life as I did during the two hundred and twenty days I was down in the dark wet freezing underworld, days that were imaginary because I had invented time down there. I had invented time and filled it with busyness and distractions. The Earth was by then wildly out of orbit of the sun, and thus without day or night of any realistic or measurable kind. And the best and worst of this dark night was that I was literally swimming in ignorance. I was at the edge of all knowledge. But we humans came into being two thousand millennia ago, and began to record things only six millennia ago. So ninety seven percent of history is lost anyway. And then I saw it.

I almost missed it. Then a sensor went off. I saw the blue. The sensor gave me an image of the spectrum. And there it was. A blue light in the midst of an absolute black. I followed the light. I was that moth. I turned the ship round and headed toward the blue blue blue. After an imaginary day and an equally imaginary night and then another nine hours of an equally imaginary day, I had found something, or rather *Lucifer* had. The light began to cover the ship. As it did, I saw that beneath the light there was a substance, a deep blue something, like a soup that enveloped and then dissolved the hull of the ship, burning away the metal with such ease I backed away from it horrified, screaming, shocked that I was not experiencing an instant death from the weight and sub-zero temperatures of the waters all around. But I wasn't. Perhaps the blue was denser and stronger than the water. Perhaps it could withstand the pressure. I knew no science for what was happening, so I will describe what I remember:

In the beginning there was the light. Then the light grew denser. The deep blue something melted the hull. It ate into everything. As it came to get me, I tried to escape. But there is no escape from the light. There never is. It got me. I was swallowed whole, immersed in this blue substance that seemed fluidic, but as if it was seething with life itself. As it subsumed me, my body began to dissolve. My skin fell away and I stood staring at my muscles and blood vessels, until they too were erased. My organs, my skin, my nails, my blood, my bones, everything I could say constituted who I thought I was, was gone, and the shock and the horror I experienced was embodied in my screams, screams that were snuffed out because I was simply not there. All my life I thought I was my body, but somehow I wasn't. I was something else as well as the body. I had been downloaded into a pure energy being, or at least something that was no longer human, if one can say a human is its human body. So the blue light killed me. This was how I died and yet did not die. All of the times I had brilliantly evaded death were reduced to this one moment of great irony. I no longer saw or heard or touched or felt. Information permeated me. The waves and shimmerings of the tiny energetic fibers that held all that is, or was, resonated in my being, attuning me to reality, the sounds and signals that emanate beneath and between the mundanities that make up so much of my life. I had dissolved out of time and emerged into space time. All of the thousand torments that had impressed themselves upon me seemed trivial. I swam in the ocean of forgetting. All the awful trivialities that had ruined my peace were lost. Like the Earth as I knew it, they had left. Being no longer limited by time or space, I was infinitely unbored. And so i came to the end. I am here. At the bottom of the ocean. There is life here. And yet i am here and not here. I am here with you as you see this. Hello. Don't be. No fear. Don't be anything. There is nothing here. No envy, malice, hate. This is an end to all things. In this there is freedom. In death there is life. A beginning and an end.

Fear & Fantasy

BEYOND THE CENTRE

WRITERS IN THEIR OWN WORDS

EDITED BY **DECLAN MEADE**

AN IRISH WRITERS CENTRE ANTHOLOGY

A landmark anthology of essays by some of Ireland's foremost contemporary writers – specially commissioned to mark the 25th anniversary of the Irish Writers Centre.

'As soon as we took possession of Number 19 we could feel the power of the place' – *PETER SIRR*

'The working-class writer is obliged to steel herself to ignore the class barriers in the arts' – *LISA McINERNEY*

'Sometimes writing no longer seems like the thing I do, it seems like the thing I am' – *KEVIN BARRY*

Published by New Island and available from all good bookstores this autumn or online at www.newisland.ie

Irish Writers Centre — Áras Scríbhneoirí na hÉireann

NEW ISLAND

NOTES ON CONTRIBUTORS

Oliver Arnoldi is a writer, journalist and documentary filmmaker who recently graduated from Columbia University. He is from London and works for *VICE* on HBO in Brooklyn, New York.

Peter Bachev (b.1989) holds a largely superfluous Master's in Gender Studies (LSE), co-ordinates sex education provision in secondary schools across London and is, shockingly, *not* writing his first novel.

Natasha Calder studied English at Trinity College Dublin and later at Cambridge University. She now works as a technical writer in the cyber security industry.

Evan Costigan is a winner of the Boyle Poetry Competition, Francis Ledwidge Poetry Award and was shortlisted for the Hennessy award for poetry in 2014. Poems have been published in numerous publications.

Darragh Cotter is from west Limerick. This is his first published story. He lives in Bucharest.

Patrick Cotter has been published in the *Awl*, the *Financial Times*, *PN Review*, *Poetry*, *Poetry Review* & elsewhere. He has published two full collections, a verse novella and several chapbooks. www.patrickcotter.ie

Trevor Fevin recently completed an MA in creative writing at Edge Hill University. He has previously been published in *St Sebastian Review* and *Best British Short Stories 2016*.

Ronan Flaherty's stories have appeared in *Crannóg, The South Circular, HeadStuff* and *The Penny Dreadful*. He is currently working on a collection of short stories. He lives in Dublin.

Jonathan Greenhause won the 2015 Editor's Choice Poetry Award from Kind of a Hurricane Press and his poems have appeared in *LitMag, The Moth, The Poetry Bus,* and *Southword Journal*.

Anne Griffin has been shortlisted for a Hennessy award and longlisted for the Seán Ó Faoláin award. She is currently completing her first novel, *All That I Have Been*.

Gerard Hanberry has published four collections of poetry, most recently *What Our Shoes Say About Us* (Salmon Poetry, 2014). His most recent non-fiction work *At Raglan Road – Great Irish Love Songs and the Women Who Inspired Them* (The Collins Press) was published in September of this year.

Caroline Hardaker lives in the northeast of England and her poetry has been published worldwide. Her debut collection, *Eye, Tongue, Machinus*, will be released with Goya Press in 2017.

Alex Harper's poetry has appeared in *Cordite Poetry Review*, *The Interpreter's House*, and *Liminality*, among others. He lives in England and can be found on Twitter as @harpertext.

Olivia Heal is a writer and translator from French. Her most recent translation was collected in *Best European Fiction 2016*. She is doing a Creative-Critical PhD at UEA.

James B.L. Hollands was born in London but now lives at the other end of the world with his partner and his puppy, both of whom he loves very much.

Clara Kumagai's writing has appeared in *Banshee*, *Room*, *Event*, and *Icarus*, and she is currently completing a young adult novel. She is from Ireland, Canada, and Japan.

Simon Lewis was the 2015 winner of the Hennessy award for poetry and runner-up in the Patrick Kavanagh Award. His first collection, *Jewtown*, is published by Doire Press.

Siobhán McGibbon is a visual artist interested in the intersections between art and science. Her practice explores the 'The modern Prometheus' through a series of investigations in sectors of medical exploration.

David McLoghlin is the author of *Waiting for Saint Brendan and Other Poems* (Salmon Poetry, 2012). His second collection, *Santiago Sketches*, is forthcoming from Salmon in 2017.

Paul McMahon's debut chapbook will be published by Southword Editions in November. Awards include The Keats-Shelley, The Ballymaloe International, The Nottingham Open, The Westport, and The Golden Pen.

Susan Millar DuMars has published four poetry collections with Salmon; the most recent, *Bone Fire*, was published in April 2016. Susan and her husband have coordinated the Over the Edge readings series in Galway since 2003.

Bernice M. Murphy is the director of the MPhil in Popular Literature at Trinity College Dublin. She has published many books and articles on topics related to horror film and fiction.

Brendan Murphy's fiction has appeared in journals and anthologies in Ireland and the UK. His play, *Kicking Oscar's Corpse,*was performed at the Town Hall Theatre, Galway, in 2015. He is currently working on a collection of short stories.

Roisín O'Donnell's short stories have appeared in journals internationally and feature in the anthologies *Young Irelanders, The Long Gaze Back* and *The Glass Shore*. Her debut collection, *Wild Quiet,* was published in 2016. She lives in Dublin.

Maeve O'Lynn completed her PhD on Gender and Genre in NI Fiction at Ulster University in 2011. As a writer and researcher, her primary interests have been liminality, transition, horror, gender and the unheimlich. Maeve has published work in *Fortnight, Estudios Irlandeses* and *The Honest Ulsterman*. She began collaborating on The Xenophon Project with visual artist Siobhán McGibbon in summer 2015; they are currently working on phase two.

Nessa O'Mahony's most recent poetry book was *Her Father's Daughter* (Salmon Poetry, 2014). She is co-editor with Siobhan Campbell of *Inside History*, a book of poems and essays on Eavan Boland (Arlen House, 2017).

Heather Parry is a writer and editor who lives in Edinburgh. She writes dark, surrealist short fiction and is currently working on her first novel.

Rachel Plummer has had poems published in magazines including *Mslexia* and *Agenda*. She is a recipient of the Scottish Book Trust New Writer Award for poetry. Find her at www.rachelplummer.co.uk

Vladimir Poleganov is a Bulgarian writer. His work has been published in Dalkey Archive Press's *Best European Fiction 2016, Granta Bulgaria, The Drunken Boat* and others.

Niamh Prior's writing has appeared in journals including *Quarryman, Southword* and *The Penny Dreadful*. She is undertaking a PhD in Creative Writing at UCC, funded by the Irish Research Council.

Jane Robinson lives in Dublin. Her poems have been published in *The Level Crossing, The Interpreter's House, Abridged, Southword, Magma* and *Poetry Ireland Review*, and awarded the Strokestown and Red Line Poetry Prize.

Dave Rudden is the author of the critically-acclaimed bestseller *Knights of the Borrowed Dark*. He enjoys cats, adventure and being cruel to fictional children.

Oran Ryan's novels include *The Death of Finn*, *Ten Short Novels by Arthur Kruger* and *One-Inch Punch*. He has written plays for the stage and radio as well as publishing poetry and short stories. He regularly contributes literary criticism to magazines at home and abroad.

Luke Sheehan was born and raised in Dublin. He has worked as an editor, writer and teacher in Ireland, France, Lebanon and China. He currently resides in Shanghai.

Ian Shine's stories have appeared in publications including *Litro*, *Firewords* and the National Flash Fiction Day anthologies for 2013-16. He is currently working on a short story collection.

Philip St John's latest play, *Temptress* (2015), will be restaged in Dublin next year. His stories have appeared in *New Irish Writing* and elsewhere. He has twice received Arts Council literature bursaries.

Matthew Sweeney's most recent collection, *Inquisition Lane*, was published by Bloodaxe in October 2015. His previous collection, *Horse Music* (Bloodaxe, 2013), won the inaugural Piggott Poetry Prize from Listowel Writers' Week.

Lucy Sweeney Byrne writes short fiction and essays. Her work has appeared in magazines such as *Banshee* and the 'In the Wake of the Rising' issue of *The Stinging Fly*. Lucy lives in Dublin, and is currently working on a book.

Jennie Taylor is a curator and writer from Dublin currently based in Brooklyn, New York. She has curated group and solo exhibitions in spaces including The Joinery, Monster Truck Gallery and The Mart.

Rachel Sneyd is a Dublin-based YA writer. She has worked in politics, education and the non-profit sector. She reviews children's books for *Inis* and Gobblefunked.com.

Dawn Watson is a writer from Belfast. She has been published in *The Moth*, *The Vacuum* and *The Honest Ulsterman*. Dawn is a former tabloid sub-editor.

~

Our guest editor:

Mia Gallagher is the author of two acclaimed novels: *HellFire* (Penguin Ireland, 2006) which received the Irish Tatler Literature Award in 2007, and *Beautiful Pictures of the Lost Homeland* (New Island, 2016). Her short fiction has been published internationally and she has received several literature bursaries from the Arts Council. 'Fear & Fantasy' is her editorial debut.